D.M. PAGE

Bound

Brickstone University Reverse Harem Book 2

Copyright © 2024 by D.M. Page

All rights reserved. No part of this publication may be reproduced, stored or transmitted in any form or by any means, electronic, mechanical, photocopying, recording, scanning, or otherwise without written permission from the publisher. It is illegal to copy this book, post it to a website, or distribute it by any other means without permission.

This novel is entirely a work of fiction. The names, characters and incidents portrayed in it are the work of the author's imagination. Any resemblance to actual persons, living or dead, events or localities is entirely coincidental.

D.M. Page asserts the moral right to be identified as the author of this work.

D.M. Page has no responsibility for the persistence or accuracy of URLs for external or third-party Internet Websites referred to in this publication and does not guarantee that any content on such Websites is, or will remain, accurate or appropriate.

Designations used by companies to distinguish their products are often claimed as trademarks. All brand names and product names used in this book and on its cover are trade names, service marks, trademarks and registered trademarks of their respective owners. The publishers and the book are not associated with any product or vendor mentioned in this book. None of the companies referenced within the book have endorsed the book.

Second edition

*This book was professionally typeset on Reedsy.
Find out more at reedsy.com*

Contents

1	Jay	1
2	Aly	7
3	Aly	17
4	Aly	22
5	Jeremy	26
6	Aly	30
7	Aly	35
8	Kiran	39
9	Aly	43
10	Aly	48
11	Aly	53
12	Aly	59
13	Aly	65
14	Ajax	71
15	Aly	76
16	Aly	80
17	Jay	84
18	Aly	88
19	Aly	93
20	Aly	98
21	Nicoli	105
22	Aly	109
23	Aly	116
24	Aly	123

25 Aly	131
26 Aly	138
27 Aly	143
28 Aly	149
29 Jeremy	154
30 Ajax	158
About the Author	162
Also by D.M. Page	164

One

Jay

After Nic removed the spell from Aly and Jeremy revealed his new mating mark, Aly was completely unconscious. I grabbed and settled her into my lap, feeling the urge to get her away from Nic and Jeremy. We've been sitting here in a stare-off for what feels like a while.

"How could you mate her without her permission?" Kiran finally breaks the silence by asking. It's the question I think we all have for Nic and Jeremy.

By combining Jeremy and Aly's blood, they completed their mating bond. They are forever bound together and Aly had no choice in it.

"We had to. She was going to die without Jeremy's blood. We didn't have a choice, and I think she would rather be alive than have had a choice," Nic responds calmly.

I know he's telling the truth and being reasonable, but I can't help being furious for Aly.

Bound

"There was no other way?" Jax asks softly.

Nic shakes his head no. "Do you really think I would have suggested it if there was? I care about her just as much as you guys do. I'm her mate, too."

And he's right, which takes the wind out of my sails. I know how hard a decision that had to be for him and Jeremy. We all calm down and my anger is replaced with jealousy. More than anything, I am grateful Aly is okay and grateful Jeremy and Nic saved her, but I'm jealous Jeremy is mated to her when I'm not. Aly and I actually have a relationship, Jeremy has only been a dick to her.

There's nothing I can do about it now, I'll just have to work hard to be the mate Aly deserves so she wants to bond with me too.

An hour later, Aly is still unconscious in my arms. The five of us are huddled around her. We have barely moved since Nic finished the spell.

"Why isn't she waking up?" I ask, rubbing at the nape of my neck.

"She should wake up soon. It's not an exact science and her body went through a lot," Nic answers for the tenth time, pressing his fingers to the bridge of his nose. We all keep asking him every few minutes like the answer will have changed—everyone except Jeremy, who now has a direct line to her.

Jeremy can probably feel what's going on, can feel that she's still alive and breathing. That nothing else has gone wrong while we just sit here. He knows all the things we can only tell from examining her on the outside.

He keeps reaching up and touching his chest, where the new mark is. I think he's doing it subconsciously, but each time he does it, he momentarily strengthens their connection. It's

Jay

probably reassuring him each time.

I gaze back down at her lying in my arms. It appears like she's just sleeping, but without any twitching or movement, it feels more like she's dead. The only reason I am calm at all is because I can see her chest moving and hear her heart beating.

I know none of us expected things to go this way. Who could have guessed Aly would have had a powerful memory spell on her, programmed to make her forget anything supernatural? And that the spell would be too intense for Nic to break alone. It's clear there is more to her story than we know, probably more than she knows. She must be something supernatural, like we expected, and perhaps it's hidden under more spells. But why would someone need to put these spells on her in the first place? It almost killed her when Nic tried to remove it. Why would someone risk that?

I look up at Jeremy, the moody fucker, who has spent the whole time we've known her denying any interest in her. And he is the first one to be fully mated to her. I have no idea how we are going to explain all this to her now. It just got ten times more complicated. At least if it had been one of the four of us, it would have been slightly easier.

"Is there any way to wake her up quicker?" Kiran asks, his voice shaking as he looks at Nic.

He thinks about it for a minute but shakes his head no. "We should let her wake up naturally. There's too many variables we don't know about. If she had a spell that big on her, there's a chance she has others."

I guess we followed the same thought process about the possibility of more spells.

"Can't you check that?" Jax asks.

But again, Nic shakes his head. "Whoever put that first spell on her was stronger than me. Until I have more supplies and do some research I won't be able to check."

We all look back down at Aly. I drop a quick kiss on her forehead and whisper, "Wake up, Aly Kat. We are all worried about you out here."

We sit in silence again for another few minutes, each of us lost in our thoughts.

"How are we going to tell her about everything *now*?" Jax asks, breaking my thought process.

Jeremy appears like he's about to speak up for the first time, but Nic cuts him off with a sharp glare. "We have to tell her everything, no holding anything back. She's going to look down and see the mark and have a million questions if we don't."

"You could hide it with magic, Nic," Jeremy mumbles, bowing his head and looking away.

"No, we aren't lying to our mate anymore. She would still feel the effects of the mate bond, even if she didn't see the mark, Jer," Kiran says firmly, and I agree entirely.

"You're going to have to talk to her," I add, addressing Jeremy. He nods, leaning back against the wall, looking resigned to his fate.

"Would you really want to hide from this? You've been given a gift from fate, don't spit in fate's face," Jax says, giving Jeremy a hard glare.

Jeremy gazes up at all of us, with the most vulnerable expression I've ever seen on his face.

"She's not going to want me, and she's completely stuck. She didn't have a choice, but if she did, I wouldn't be it," he says, and his voice sounds weak.

I knew Jeremy had big feelings under all that ice, but he rarely

Jay

lets them out. He must be pretty scared to have voiced it aloud.

"You'd be surprised, Jer. I'm not saying you won't have some ground to make up and some apologies to give, but I think Aly already likes you. Show her you like her too, and I think you guys will be okay," Nic reassures him.

"Yeah, just don't fuck up and make it worse. She needs you now more than ever. You've had time to come to terms with things. She didn't get any," Kiran adds giving him a pointed look.

Jeremy deflates and joins us on the floor around her. He reaches out and pushes the hair back from her forehead, then whispers, "I won't fuck it up."

And I think he means that. I think he's going to try and be the mate she deserves as she navigates through this new landscape. Hopefully, with all of us around her, she'll realize what a gift this is.

She starts to stir in my arms, and we all gaze down, hoping she's waking up. She doesn't open her eyes, but it's a positive sign.

"Do you think she'll wake up soon?" I ask with wide eyes.

"Yeah, I think she will," Jeremy responds.

Kiran stands up, pulling Jax with him, and I'm surprised. Don't they want to be here when she wakes up? I consider them, raising a brow in question, and Kiran responds.

"She might be hungry or thirsty when she wakes up. She's been out for a while, and we don't know how this has affected her. We are going to make her some food, just in case. Tell us if she wakes up while we are gone, okay?"

I smile at their thoughtfulness and nod my head yes.

With Aly still in my arms, I scoot backward so my back is against the wall and lean on it to get more comfortable. I run my fingers through her hair, willing her to wake up for me.

She stirs again without fully waking up, but it makes me hopeful she will soon.

Nic and Jeremy stand across the room, stretching some after being on the floor for so long.

They lower their voices, but with my shifter hearing, I can still hear Jeremy asking Nic how he should act around her. Damn, he is nervous. We are all nervous, but he has a lot more on the line now. And he wasn't her favorite person to start with. At least if it was one of us four we would have already been in a relationship.

Two

Aly

I'm waking up from what feels like the brink of death. My limbs are groggy, and it feels like they weigh one hundred pounds. My mouth is so dry it feels like I swallowed sandpaper, and my ears are ringing. What is going on?

The last thing I remember is being over at the guys' house. They were acting so weird and clearly had something they wanted to talk to me about. I remember feeling like they were going to make me choose, but it's all black after that. Did I pass out from the shock of their news or something? I try really hard to remember, but it feels like those memories are lost to a black hole, never to be recovered. Trying to remember causes sharp pain to shoot through my head, making me feel even worse.

I wonder if they'll tell me what they said or what happened. I trust them, but they may be sheepish if this is how I reacted the first time.

Nic, Jay, Kiran, Ajax, and even Jeremy came out of nowhere this year. They bulldozed right into my life and integrated me into their little group. We've only known each other briefly, but it honestly feels like they've been part of my life forever.

What if they did say I had to choose, and this is how I reacted? I've shared intimate moments with a lot of them, and they seemed like they didn't mind sharing, but how could they not? What guy would be willing to share their girl, even if it is with their best friends?

My mind is racing a mile a minute and I know I need to open my eyes and deal with whatever happened. I brace myself then peel my eyes open and it feels like sharp knives behind my eyes, as the brightness of the room seeps in.

When my vision finally clears, I see Jay cradling me in his arms. His focus isn't on me, though. He's staring at something else in front of him, which gives me a moment to search him for clues.

He appears as attractive as ever with his huge frame, bulging muscles and gorgeous face but what's missing is his signature smile. It takes a lot to bring Jay down but right now he looks like a mixture of angry and scared. His hold on me is protective, though, so hopefully he's not upset with me.

It takes me another few minutes to make my mouth work. It feels like my body shut down on me and is learning how to function again.

"What's going on?" I croak through the sandpaper in my throat.

His eyes shoot down at me, and a look of relief spreads through his features. I guess he was scared for me. I wonder how long I was out.

"Oh, Aly Kat, you're okay!" he shouts, and I wince. A guilty

Aly

grimace comes over his face, and he leans in closer to whisper much softer, "I'm sorry. I'm just so relieved to see you awake."

"What happened, Jay?" I ask again, a rasp to my voice.

He appears nervous, and instead of answering me, he gazes up and away from me to someone else.

I slowly turn my head to see Nic and Jeremy watching us from across the room. My neck is incredibly stiff as I try to move it. It looks like they're having an intense discussion with just their eyes, but it's hard to tell from here. What don't they want to tell me?

I can feel myself getting worked up and nervous. My heart starts beating faster, and my breathing becomes shorter until I'm on the verge of a panic attack.

Jeremy shoots out of his seat, landing at my side. He reaches out a hand towards me, but at the last second, he thinks better of it and pulls it back.

"Aly, you have to relax, okay? We will explain everything, and it's all going to be okay. Deep breaths, breathe with me."

Then he starts taking deep, emphasized breaths in and out, encouraging me to join in. I try to copy him, and eventually, I come down some, to the point where I'm no longer on the verge of completely losing it. Why is Jeremy helping me?

"You're in pain," Jeremy says, not a question but a statement, and then peers over at Nic.

Nic looks surprised by this, too, but he leans over and rests a hand on my head until I start to feel better and can think more easily.

"What did you just do?" I ask Nic.

Instead of answering my question, he asks me one of his own. "What do you remember, Aly?"

"I remember getting here and being nervous about what you

had to tell me. And since I still don't know and I was just unconscious, I'm more concerned," I respond.

Nic nods and gazes back at me with a soft smile.

"I'll explain everything in a minute. Let's wait for Kiran and Ajax to come back. When you started waking up, they went downstairs to make something for you to eat and get water. They should be back any minute, okay?"

"Okay," I whisper.

Jay nuzzles closer to me and drops a kiss right on my lips, chaste and sweet. His expression is a little manic as he observes me. How long was I out for him to be so worried? Even Jeremy is scared, so it must have been bad.

"It's okay, Jay. I'm here. I'm awake, so it'll all be fine," I reassure him, even though I'm the one in the dark. But I have an urge to erase the panic from his eyes.

Kiran and Jax pick that moment to come back in the room, and when they see I'm awake, they rush over.

"Oh baby, I'm so glad you're awake!" Kiran says while he drops next to me on the floor.

Jax sits next to him and holds out a glass. "Here, Aly, drink some water."

I attempt to sit up in Jay's lap, but he's got a death grip on me, so it takes him maneuvering me to make it happen. Once I'm up, I take the glass from Jax. The cool water feels incredible on my throat and I'm grateful they thought to get it for me.

My stomach chooses that moment to rumble out loud, and I give a sheepish look to Kiran, who's holding the food.

"Here." He passes over a plate. "It's some toast with peanut butter and jelly. If that doesn't sound good, I can always make something else. I think we have…"

But I cut him off. "This is great, perfect, really. Thank you."

Aly

I lean forward and kiss both him and Jax on the cheek before settling back against Jay.

I take a few bites of my toast, then stare at Nic expectantly. He sighs before joining us all on the floor.

"This is going to be a shock, but please just hear us out before coming to any conclusions, okay?" He asks.

Maybe whatever they already tried to tell me was such a shock I passed out. But why did my body feel like death if it was just that?

"Okay," I respond.

Nic hesitates a second, then takes a deep breath before starting.

"Supernaturals exist, some of the species you've probably seen in television or movies are real. Although, Hollywood gets it wrong a lot."

He gives me a second to digest that before continuing. Am I shocked to find out they're real? Yes. But I guess it's not so crazy to believe that these tales have some truth behind them. But does Nic know this for sure, or is he saying he's a believer? Oh no, are they in some weird believer cult, and they want me to join?

"Do you have proof?" I ask slowly.

He nods. "Yes, we have proof because *we* are supernatural. I'm a mage, so I could show you some magic right now if you want?"

I can feel my eyes grow huge at that. The idea of *them* being supernatural is insane. I've never seen anything that would hint at that, and we have spent a lot of time together. They would have slipped up and shown me something unexplainable. They could be insane, and I just never realized. That seems more likely than this.

But, he asked me to hear them out so instead of voicing my doubt, I give him a chance to prove his sanity by nodding yes.

He conjures real fire in his hand right in front of me. I can feel the heat coming off it and everything. My jaw drops, and he lets out a little laugh. Holy shit, he is a mage. He must have used magic to heal me when I first woke up. That's why I felt better so quickly.

I realize he said they were all supernatural, but he didn't say 'we' are mages, so what are the rest of them?

I peer around, expectantly, at each of them.

Kiran starts first, speaking so fast it's almost hard to understand, "I'm a dark fae, which doesn't mean I'm evil like lore may suggest. It just means I draw power from negative emotions."

I nod, accepting that right away. Kiran is far from evil. He's never shown me anything dark since I've known him. I smile at him and he looks relieved that I believe him right away. Note to self, he is nervous about my reaction to him being a dark fae.

I move to Jax next, drawing a conclusion, "So you must be a dark fae too, right? Since you're twins."

He appears uncomfortable but answers me anyway, "Actually, I'm a light fae, and it's incredibly rare that, as twins, we aren't the same species."

I'm sure I'll have more questions about that later, but for now, I'm just trying to absorb the basics. I already feel like my brain is going to explode, and I can sense they have a lot more to tell me.

I scan Jay, and he shares, "I'm a wolf shifter."

I'm more familiar with that one. It's popular in the media, and I've seen movies or read books with wolf shifters in them.

"You are? Can I see you shift one day?" I ask.

Aly

He perks up at that. "Yes, of course, my wolf is dying to meet you up close." He leans in conspiratorially. "I'm not the only one with an alternate form, so you'll have to see them shift for you too."

I smile at that and give them all a sweet expression, which they respond to with a nod.

"Another time, though," Nic says, and I agree because, again, I'm feeling like it's already too much.

Lastly, I focus on Jeremy, wondering if he will tell me. He looks uncertain, and for once, it seems like he's nervous, not that he doesn't want to.

Kiran nudges him, and finally, he blurts out, "Demon, I'm a demon."

I can't help it, I burst out laughing and he looks shocked.

"Oh my God, of course! Is that why you're so moody and broody all the time?" I ask.

He scowls at me, and it's then I realize I just insulted a *demon* who doesn't like me. Shit, I don't know anything about actual demons, but that seems like a terrible idea. Instead of smiting me on the spot, he rolls his eyes and I remember that while Jeremy might not like me, he's never hurt me. I don't think he ever would.

"Okay, so you're supernatural. I believe you, and I want to know more, but this is pretty overwhelming. Can we stop for today, and maybe I can learn more in smaller spurts?" I ask.

Their faces drop instantly, and they all appear guilty.

"I wasn't saying you guys did anything wrong. I'm so glad you told me. I just want to take it slow. Is that okay?" I say quickly to try to fix their mood, but it doesn't improve.

"It's not that. I would love to say yes and let you go and digest for now, but Aly, we need to tell you more immediately.

Bound

Otherwise, you'll have questions when you realize some things and don't have answers. Can you push through a little longer?" Nic asks.

Oddly enough, they're all glancing over at Jeremy to see how he's taking things, but he's just stone-faced as usual. Why are they worried about him? It's possible he didn't want me to know this about them.

"Okay, I trust your judgment. Let's keep going," I say, and Nic smiles approvingly.

"Aly, in the supernatural community, we have these things called mates. Sometimes they're portrayed in the media, but of course, they get things wrong. Have you ever heard of them?" Nic asks.

My heart starts pounding in my chest at the mention of mates. Has one of them found theirs, and are they trying to let me down easily?

"Yeah, I guess I know a little. They're your perfect match, right? The person made for you?" As I ask, I gaze around at them, and they all give me serious expressions as I say it.

Nic smiles at that and nods. "Yes, except you're talking in the singular sense, which is one of the things the media has gotten wrong. We mate in groups, usually multiple males to one female."

My heart starts pounding with that tidbit of information. "Are you using me as practice for when you share a mate?!" I shout, enraged at the idea.

They all balk at me like I've slapped them.

"No, no, calm down. You've got it wrong, Aly. We would never do that," Kiran starts, but I'm too mad to let him keep going. It all makes sense now.

"Why not? Why else would you want to share me, if not for

Aly

practice?" I shout, trying to get out of Jay's lap.

But he doesn't let me. He bands his arms around me until I can't move.

Nic leans in and grabs my face, making me look into his eyes as he says, "Aly, we want to share you because you *are* our mate. We already know it's you."

I deflate at that, anger replaced by shock once again. I'm their *mate*? The person destined for them? Then why were they looking around guiltily and watching Jeremy's reaction?

Oh. "But not Jeremy's?" I ask, avoiding looking at him.

I'm staring at Nic, who winces as I say it, but before he gets a chance to respond, someone pulls my chin away from him and to the other side.

I'm staring right into Jeremy's eyes as he says, "You're my mate too. I'm sorry I ever made you doubt that."

And for a second, I'm not mad about how he's treated me. He looks so earnest and honest staring at me right now. But then he leans back, and the spell is broken. My walls start building back up again.

"Okay, is that everything?" I ask.

And once again, they share a guilty look.

"No, there's more. I'm sorry, Aly." Nic looks a lot more sorry than I would expect for that statement.

"Let's take a break," Kiran suggests. I love that he can tell I need it.

Nic looks ready to object, but to my surprise, Jeremy steps in. "She's overwhelmed. She needs a break, or she might lose it."

Nic nods, then turns back to me. "Can you please stay through dinner so we can continue after? I just don't want you trying to leave before we finish."

Bound

"Yes, I promise I'll stay."

Three

Aly

We start heading downstairs to the kitchen and the guys are all being super careful around me.

Jay runs ahead of me to open any door, Kiran keeps staring at me and smiling, Jax keeps stealing peeks when he thinks I'm not paying attention, Nic is dead silent and Jeremy is completely ignoring me.

Some part of me wants to go reassure Jeremy, give him a hug, or hold his hand, but that's crazy. I'm the one whose whole world was blown up. Shouldn't I want reassurance and affection instead of giving it out? Plus, experience would tell me he wouldn't want that from me, but for some reason, I feel like he needs it.

When we get to the kitchen, Jay pulls up to the fridge and asks, "Does anything sound good, Aly Kat?"

"What were you planning on having?" I ask.

"Burgers?" He says it as a question. Like, if I don't want

burgers that's the thing that's going to send me over the edge. If it wasn't the fact that they are supernatural, I don't think it'll be burgers that do it.

While I am feeling overwhelmed, these guys seem to think I'm about to lose it completely. Is that what happened before? It doesn't seem like me but I have no idea what happened. That must be what else they need to tell me.

"Burgers sound great," I say, and I try to come across as strong and reasonable, but I'm not sure I hit the mark.

Jay starts cooking, and the rest of us make our way to the table to wait. Burgers are a quick and easy meal, so it shouldn't take long.

They all awkwardly stand around the table, waiting for me to choose where I'm going to sit first. I don't think we've ever been this weird around each other, even when we were strangers at the bar.

Some part of me wants to end up next to Jeremy, but I squash that feeling and choose a random seat. Why am I obsessed with Jeremy right now?

I've always liked him, even when he's been a jerk. But right now, I feel a little obsessed, and it's weird. Is it something about knowing he's a demon? Is he using his powers or something to make me feel like this?

I would call him out and ask but if he's not, then I'll sound like a loon. And I don't think I want them all knowing I'm feeling this way. The five of us were just forming something and I still feel as strongly about them. I don't want them to get the wrong idea about things. Although, if we are all 'mates' they're probably expecting it. I guess I have no idea what the expectation is now.

Plus, Jeremy would tease me mercilessly about feeling this

Aly

way. I would never move past it if I told them how I'm feeling.

He is pointedly ignoring me, more than usual. There isn't even a snide comment thrown out, which is his typical style. It's bizarre and has me more on edge.

We all sit around the table in silence, just the sounds of Jay cooking fill the space. Of course, Kiran can't let the silence go on too long.

"So, what did everyone get on the math test?" he asks as if that's a completely normal topic to bring up.

And with a start, I realize that it is. What we've been talking about has been the weird, the abnormal.

I burst out laughing, and it's a little hysterical, but it makes me feel better and melts the tension in the room. I actually feel joy, and I'm grateful to Kiran for that. He always knows how to lighten the mood. How could he ever be something with the word 'dark' in it?

Out of the corner of my eye, I see Jeremy's shoulders drop and he seems to relax some too. That makes me feel even better for some reason.

Seeing me laugh must encourage the rest of them because they all join in.

"I got a 92," Nic says.

"86," Jeremy tosses out.

"87, ha!" Jay gloats.

I study Jax and Kiran, who are left.

"82, and I'm happy about it," Kiran says downright gleeful. I'm excited for him, I know he was nervous. I helped him study and I'm proud of how well he did.

Jax and I are in a little bit of a stare-off, clearly wondering which of us did better. My bets are on Jax but I did do incredibly well.

"Oh, just spit it out already, you nerds!" Jay comments from the kitchen.

"Fine, I got a 98," I say, and the tiny twitch in the corner of Ajax's cheek lets me know he won before he says anything.

"Damn it! What did you get, Jax?" I ask, throwing my hands up.

His smile becomes full-blown, but he doesn't rub it in. He just casually says, "99."

And even though I lost, it makes me smile. Because this feels more like the guys I'm used to. The guys who are my best friends, who I can trust. It's not the awkward group we were a few minutes ago.

Jay brings over a pile of burgers and places one on my plate before taking one for himself. Once he's done, the rest of them dig in. It was sweet he served me first, even though he cooked.

We all eat, and after I finish my first, I realize Jay is on his fourth. He catches me staring with a raised brow, so he explains.

"I've, uh, been downplaying how much I eat in front of you, but now that you know I'm a wolf, you should know I eat like one too. I'm always hungry."

Nic chimes in, "We all eat more than humans. Although, Jay eats the most. We haven't noticed if you do?" He ended that on a question clearly for me to answer. Does he think I might be supernatural, too?

"Uh, I don't think I do. Are you asking because you think I'm not human? If I eat a normal amount, would that mean I'm not supernatural?"

"We don't know, Aly. It could mean something is repressing your supernatural side. We think someone doesn't want you to know about it. We can look into it. Let's wait and talk about

Aly

it after dinner," Nic responds, and I'm glad to have him, them, on my side.

I'm not sure if I want to be only human or not, but a small part of me wonders what it would be like to be supernatural.

We finish up dinner with some small talk and it's so nice I almost forget there's more to discuss. I was just starting to digest some of this information, but now I need to get more handed to me.

We are all staring down at empty plates, avoiding what comes next, but we need to address it. It's important to them that I know what else is going on.

"Should we move to the living room and finish the conversation we started?" I ask reluctantly.

They all know what I'm talking about immediately, nodding and standing up. We drop our dishes off in the kitchen and then make our way to the living room.

Four

Aly

I make my way over to the couch and sit down, the rest of them finding spots all around me. They're all waiting on me to decide when I'm ready and while I needed the break, I want to hear the rest. I need to know everything they have to tell me before I can form any real conclusions.

"Okay, let's finish, what else is there?" I ask.

Once again, they defer to Nic, and he continues, "Well, we tried to tell you about us being supernaturals before you," he pauses and sounds less sure when he continues, "passed out."

"Is that why I passed out? From shock?" I ask.

Nic shakes his head. "No, you had a memory spell on you. One designed to make you forget anything supernatural."

"Had?" I ask, my thoughts catching on that word and why I can now have this conversation if there was a spell stopping it before.

"Had," he confirms, "I removed it," he's about to continue but

Aly

I break in with my question first.

"Why would I have a spell like that on me?"

"Well, we think you're supernatural too, but we don't know what. And someone wanted to hide that from you with this spell."

Okay, my mind is officially blown. Me? A supernatural? I haven't done anything supernatural before in my life. But would I have known if I had this spell on me? I sit back, assuming this is the big bomb they need to drop, and relax back into the couch to process, but Kiran speaks up.

"There's more Aly, I'm sorry."

"More? What more could there possibly be? I have five supernatural mates who think I'm also supernatural, and someone put a spell on me so I wouldn't realize it!" I'm shouting, a little hysterical.

Nic and Jeremy share a look before Nic continues.

"I know it's a lot. I'm sorry Aly. It was a complicated spell to remove, and once I started, I had to finish it. But, it didn't go smoothly, and you started to die on us from the strain of it. Whoever put this spell on you never wanted it removed, and doing so was going to kill you."

"Oh shit, so I didn't pass out, I almost died?" I ask.

"Yes, and it was terrifying for all of us," Jay responds, his eyes haunted.

"So why didn't I die?" I whisper.

"Demon blood is incredibly powerful in a spell and even has healing properties, so by adding Jeremy's blood to yours, we were able to save you," Nic adds, facing Jeremy, who looks like he might pass out.

He's so white that he might be sick. I've never seen him like this. Why is he so uncomfortable with being the person who saved me?

"Okay." I turn to Jeremy. "Thank you for saving me. Why do you all seem like this is the worst part?"

No one answers me, all waiting on Jeremy. When he doesn't say anything, I wait for Nic to explain, but he's just giving Jeremy a cutting look.

"Uh," Jeremy starts, "Aly, the thing is, we may all be your mates, but we have to bond you for it to be official."

That actually makes me relax some. It felt like a lot to suddenly be mated to five guys, and this means we have more time to get to know each other and decide.

I relax back in my seat at that news, and Jeremy winces. Okay, there is more. I wish he would just spit it out. These mood swings are going to give me a headache.

He sits up a little, straightening his shoulders, before saying, "And each species has different ways of mating. The way that demons mate is by," and he pauses, staring into my eyes as he says, "by sharing blood."

And it all clicks. Jeremy and I are bonded. By saving my life, he sacrificed our choice. It's something I can't be mad about, considering I would be dead, but he's unhappy about it.

He didn't want this. He was never perusing me like the other four. He was actively avoiding me, and now he doesn't have that choice. That's why everyone keeps checking on him.

A day ago, I had no idea mates existed, and now the idea that I'm mated to someone who doesn't want me breaks my heart.

I look up at Jeremy again, and he's downright miserable, clearly unhappy with things. Now it makes sense why.

I gaze around at the other guys, who look ready to crawl out of their skin. They're so uncomfortable. They know Jeremy doesn't want me, that he's unhappy, and they hate having to

Aly

watch this play out.

Why couldn't it have been one of these four who had the blood to save me? Why did fate force Jeremy's hand? Now, we're both destined to be miserable.

I stand up, slowly and carefully, until I'm sure I've got my feet under me, and the guys all shoot up around me.

"Where are you going, Aly?" Jay asks.

I start slowly backing away from them all and closer to the door.

"Wait, don't go. We can help you through this," Kiran adds.

"Stay Aly, it'll all be okay," Jax says.

"We can answer any questions you have," Nic offers.

I peer at Jeremy to see if he's going to ask me to stay, and for a second, it almost seems like he might. He lifts his arm, reaching out to me, but he drops it at the last second.

And that's the final straw. It feels like my heart is cracking.

"I've got to go," I say.

I turn around and run out the front door, hoping they don't follow me.

Five

Jeremy

"What the fuck was that?!" Jay asks, turning on me and getting in my face.

What the fuck is he yelling at me about? I'm the one who just had to feel her pain, disappointment, and heartbreak through the bond while my mate discovered we are mated.

I'm the idiot who thought I had a chance to win her over, but based on the emotions I just felt, I've got no chance.

I'm the one who just watched her run away from me, right out the door. I'm the one who had no idea what the right thing to say, to make her stay, was. Everyone else tried, but I couldn't come up with something. Everything that ran through my head was stupid and wrong and wouldn't be enough.

"She wanted you to say something! To tell her to stay or that you want her! You idiot, instead, you just stood there as she left," Kiran adds, joining Jay in facing off against me. He goes shoulder to shoulder with Jay, clearly trying to intimidate me.

Jeremy

What? She did? How would they know? I'm the one connected to her, I actually know what she was thinking, even if they wish they did.

"That's not what she wanted. She was upset about being mated to me. I'm the one who can feel her emotions through the bond!" I shout and I instantly feel bad because the guys all seem hurt by that. Some of their faces drop and some just look like they want to throttle me.

But it's the truth, even if they're jealous that she and I bonded first. Or maybe they're hurt I threw it in their faces. This emotional stuff is too much for me. I didn't deserve to be mated to her first. It's an honor, one I don't deserve.

Kiran is downright murderous and I don't think I've ever seen him live up to being a dark fae as much as right now. Usually, he's mister happy-go-lucky, but right now, if looks could kill, I'd be six feet under.

"You may have forgotten that Jax and I can feel emotions with our powers. So even if we don't have the *bond*," he emphasizes that line, letting me know what he thought of me throwing that in their faces, "we know what she's feeling."

Shit, he's right. I'm an ass, and I go to say that when I'm cut off by Jax. Jax who must be really upset to be talking this way to any of us, when he's usually the peacekeeper of the group.

"And since we have had this link to people a lot longer than you have, you might like some of our knowledge in the area. Like for example, you can feel the emotion but not the thought behind it. Various thoughts can lead to the same emotion," he finishes like I'm an idiot.

Before anyone else can jump in and berate me, I speak up, "I'm sorry, okay? I shouldn't have said that but I know what I felt. What other thoughts could make her feel disappointment, hurt, and sadness when hearing I'm her mate? She doesn't want me." The way she was looking at me when she found out killed me.

They all stare at me like I'm the biggest idiot and I'm pretty over it. I might just punch one of them in the face, so this conversation can be over, and I can go brood in peace. Be miserable in peace.

"Stop looking at me like I'm an idiot!" I shout.

"Then stop being an idiot," Kiran throws back, and this time, I lunge for him.

Before I make contact with him, I'm swallowed in a cloud of darkness, holding me hostage. It feels like it's slowly suffocating me, not enough to kill me, just enough to be painful. I know better than to attack Kiran when he's surrounded by so many negative emotions. His strength must be overflowing.

Even without the extra juice, he's incredibly powerful. He rarely uses that power, and especially not against any of us, but I pushed him too far this time—even if he was pushing me too.

Slowly, the darkness recedes, and light trickles in along with more air. When it finally clears, I stand up. I didn't realize I had fallen to the floor during that demonstration until now.

Kiran doesn't seem sorry, and I can't blame him. I lunged at him first. He's feeling pissed and protective of his mate.

"Enough," Nic declares, and we all deflate a little. I think he's about to yell at Kiran for using his powers on me, but of course, his anger is directed at me. "Jeremy, you fucked up. I can tell you don't get it so listen and listen carefully. Aly was upset because she thinks you don't want her. That she's mated to someone who regrets that decision. She doesn't know what this fully means, but she knows how you've treated her up until this point. It was written all over her face every time she looked

Jeremy

at you. Fix it."

He's serious, and when I peer at the other guys, they're all nodding their heads in agreement. They believe that, and a little hope fills my chest that she wants me, too. But if that's true, that means I hurt her once again, and she's sitting at home in pain because of me. That just won't do anymore. We are going to fix it, and she's not going to feel like this because of me ever again. I can feel how much pain she is in currently.

"I'm going to head over there and talk to her right now," I say, walking over to the door, about to head out.

"Make sure you explain the mating bond effects she will be feeling. It's important she understands what's happening," Nic commands.

None of them stop me from leaving, they all seem happy about it. So I must be doing the right thing, for once.

Ready or not, Aly, here I come.

Six

Aly

I'm power-walking away from the guys' house and back to the apartment I share with Anna. My mind is racing a mile a minute with everything the guys revealed, but it always comes back to Jeremy, most of all.

The further away I get, the more a twinge in my chest grows, urging me to go back to them. But I need some time to think, and I won't get any of that if I go back.

The cycle in my head tends to go: supernaturals exist, I might be one, mates exist, I have 5 mates and I'm already mated to Jeremy. Jeremy, who doesn't want me and has never wanted me. I wonder if a mate bond can be broken. I'll have to ask, but I have a feeling that if it could, Jeremy would have already made it happen or at least suggested it. Then, the cycle begins again.

I'm finally back at the apartment and when I open the door, I feel immediate relief to see Anna is home, sitting on the couch

Aly

in our living room.

Bailey was already at the front door, pacing and agitated as if he knew what state I was coming home in. He hops up onto my chest and gives me a lick before nuzzling me. I take comfort from him and give a few pets but right now, I need to talk this out with someone who can talk back.

Anna takes one look at me and hops up immediately.

"What's wrong? Who do I need to hurt?" She asks, already having my back before I explain anything.

I open my mouth to answer her and realize I can't. The guys trusted me with these secrets, and even if I trust Anna explicitly, it's not my secret to tell. And who knows, it's possible telling her would put her in danger, and I won't risk that.

I shift gears, sharing what I can even though it'll sound a lot more stupid without the life-changing details.

"It's Jeremy," I start, "he, he doesn't want me." I feel a tear run down my cheek.

Anna is less murderous but still worked up.

"Okay, and I thought you didn't like him either. Did something change?"

Yes! Everything changed, but how do I explain that without really explaining? I'm at a loss, but Anna takes it in stride anyway.

"Okay, so clearly you like him, and for some reason, things came to a head with you two. I know you're not telling me everything, and that's okay. If he doesn't want you, Aly, then he's an idiot. You're the most incredible girl I know and he's lucky you give him the time of day."

I sniffle back some of the tears that have leaked out and give her a small smile.

"Thanks, Anna. Can we snuggle on the couch and watch

some trashy TV while we eat ice cream?"

"Of course, you sit down, and I'll get the ice cream."

I plop down on the couch, and Bailey hops right into my lap. He is really in tune with my emotions right now and wants to make me feel better. I soak in his love and snuggle him back, and it helps.

All of a sudden, it feels like I can't breathe. A tightness forms in my chest, but when I take a breath, I can feel the air filling my lungs. What's going on?

When it finally goes away, I feel a strong sense of relief that doesn't belong to me before everything is cut off, and I feel normal again.

Maybe I'm losing my mind with everything I've been through today.

Anna and I settle in on the couch and snuggle up before putting on a random show. I feel better just having her support, even if I can't tell her everything that's going on.

I know she has my back, even without the information, she's my ride or die, and I'm so grateful for that.

There's a knock at the door, and Anna and I turn towards each other.

"Are you expecting someone?" I ask.

"No… are you?" She responds.

I shake my head no and get a burst of nervous anticipation that doesn't feel like it belongs to me.

Anna gets up to answer the door but half-closes it, blocking the view inside when she sees who it is.

"Jeremy." She turns around to face me with her eyes raised in question.

I shake my head, no, and she takes the hint.

"She's not here so." She starts to close the door but he must

Aly

stop the motion because it halts to a stop.

"Hey Anna, I know she's here, and I need to talk to her. Can you let me in, please? It's important," he says loud enough that I can hear.

Anna looks back at me again, in question, clearly showing Jeremy that I'm here but that the choice is mine. I shake my head, no, and she turns back to him.

"Nope, try again later. Bye now," she says, trying to close the door again.

I feel a burst of frustration that doesn't match how I'm feeling. Why are my emotions all over the place?

"Okay, okay, fine. Aly, when you're ready to talk, please let me know. We have a lot we need to discuss," he shouts from the doorway, making it clear he's talking about the mate bond.

He finally leaves, and I feel a tug in my chest the further he gets. A sensation the bond is causing me? I wonder what else the mate bond has in store for me?

Anna closes and locks the door, then comes to sit next to me on the couch.

"Do you want to talk about it?" She asks me.

"No," I respond, then bury my head in her shoulder and snuggle back in with her.

"Okay, I'll let you bury your head, literally, for now, but eventually, you're going to have to work through this. The guys are all best friends, and unless you're ready to ignore Nic, Jay, Kiran, and Jax too, then you're going to have to see Jeremy."

She's so smart and right, but I don't want to be logical right now.

"I will. I'll deal with it all soon, when it's a little less raw, okay?" I ask.

She wraps her arm around me and pulls me in close.

Bound

"Okay, deal. Now, back to reality TV."

Seven

Aly

I feel absolutely, completely, and utterly uncomfortable and I can't figure out why. No matter what I do, it's a sensation I can't escape.

I've tried showering, exercising, changing positions, and trying to distract myself, but nothing works. On top of that, all I can think about is Jeremy and the guys—mostly Jeremy and how he looked when I left, how he didn't want me.

It's like a shooting pain in my heart every few minutes when I think of it.

He's come by a couple more times, trying to talk with me but Anna keeps sending him away at my request. Apparently, he's getting more and more insistent every time he comes. He's also called and texted around a million times, as all the guys have, but I ignored them until eventually, I turned off my phone.

It's too much. I wanted space to figure out and think things through, on my own. I do feel a little bad when they are insistent that they need to talk to me. I wonder if there's something more they need to tell me. They're probably just worried I will tell someone but I'm not naive. I know I can't do that.

Anna has been an angel, the best, best friend a girl could ask for. Having to deal with these guys is a full-time job right now, and she's taking over all of it. They're all trying to convince her to let them talk to me but she's respecting my wishes and holding strong. After this, I owe her, at the very least, a night out.

I know she wants to go hang out with her guy but she's stayed here to be supportive. I've told her a million times to go, but she's made do with texting him instead. I don't think I deserve a best friend like her.

Bailey has been incredibly anxious, clearly mirroring my own emotions. He's an extremely empathetic dog, and I need to be careful not to let him feel too much. Anna has also been amazing at helping me take care of him. She keeps trying to calm him down with walks, but apparently, he just keeps pulling her back home.

I decide to take a nice long bath to relax, with all the works. A glass of wine, bubbles, candles, and relaxing music. Sometimes, a girl just needs an excellent bubble bath to make everything better. Once I get it all set up, I settle in and try to clear my mind, but it just keeps coming back to Jeremy. It's like I'm obsessed, and I don't understand why. Is it the mating bond? Could it be making me feel this way? It must be because I never felt this obsessed with him before. I guess, I don't know anything about it or how it's affecting me. Is there any chance that's why they are trying so hard to get a hold of me?

I shake the thoughts out of my brain. I am trying to relax

right now. I can pick them back up again after my bath. I need a chance to clear my head and shake this feeling, not overthink things and make everything worse.

I start playing with the bubbles, making little piles and blowing them around, hoping the activity will distract me. It works for a little while, but as the bubbles clear some, I see something darker under the water.

It catches my eye, but at first, I just ignore it, assuming it's a shadow. When I see it again, I clear the bubbles more to see what it is. I'm shocked to see it's *on* me.

I rinse the area, sitting up suddenly when I realize there's something on my rib. It's like a tattoo of some kind, but I don't have any tattoos. I've always wanted some, but I know that even drunk, I've never followed through on that desire.

I jump out of the bath and rush over to the mirror to get a closer look. I can see it more clearly in the mirror, but at first, I'm still not sure what it is. It reminds me of something I've seen on TV shows before, a pentagram? I quickly pull out my phone and search for it. The images that pop up are eerily similar, so I guess it's a pentagram inked into the skin over my ribs. I'm shocked. How did this get there? I continue my Google search to see what it is or means. One website tells me it's the mark of a demon, and another tells me it's how you summon a demon. So it's related to a demon of some kind?

Then it hits me, and I'm furious. This is from Jeremy! Does he know it's here? Did he do it on purpose? Is it part of the mating bond or something else? The questions all race through my head and I realize there's only one way I'm going to get answers to these questions. I need to ask the boys. Which means I need to face them and learn more about what's going on.

Bound

I want to see their faces when I ask, especially Jeremy's. I want to know what his reaction is when I ask him what this mark is. I'm not feeling warm towards him right now so I need to know he's not lying. I have to head over there in person and catch them all off guard. Then, I can find out what's going on, starting with this mark.

I lean in to poke the spot, wondering if it'll feel any different, and as soon as I do, I feel a stronger connection to Jeremy. I can feel him freaking out, his worry and stress, and for a minute, I feel bad for him. Before I realize that this *must* be a connection to him.

That confirms my assumption but there is only one way to find out for sure.

Eight

Kiran

The guys and I have been in a panic since Aly left. She ran out before we could give her all the information about the mating bond and we have no idea how she's taking it. It's torture to know your mate is struggling but to have no idea how to help her. She's ignoring our calls and texts, and anytime one of us goes to her apartment, Anna turns us away.

I try calling her again and it goes right to voicemail. I'm pretty sure she's turned her phone off.

"What are we going to do?" I ask the group, all of us gathered in the living room.

Jeremy doesn't look up from his clenched knuckles. He's been sitting in the armchair brooding between every visit he takes to her apartment. I know it's worse for him since he has the bond. Besides being apart, he's feeling how she's doing, and it's clearly not good.

"I need to go back," Jeremy finally says and he gets up and

goes right to the door to leave. No room for discussion from any of us.

Nic flicks his wrist and mutters a spell, blocking Jeremy from leaving.

"Stop. We can't keep going over there. Anna might call the cops on us or something. We are bordering on harassment at this point," Nic commands.

"I need to get closer to her," Jeremy shouts while pounding against the invisible wall Nic created. He sounds desperate, and I feel terrible for him. I've never seen him show this much emotion.

"We know," Jax says, standing up and walking over to him. "Let's make a plan then you can go. Okay?"

Jeremy gives a sharp nod, then Jax leads him back to his seat before sitting down himself.

"So we need to speak with Aly to explain what she's feeling and why but she's using Anna as a shield and probably turned her phone off," I state the problem, gazing around for a solution.

"I doubt she will miss class over this. We could catch her on campus tomorrow," Jay suggests, looking eager to finally see her.

Since Aly left, Jay has been acting like a kicked puppy. He's been smelling every change in emotion through Jeremy, and that's been making things worse and worse. He's not experiencing them, but he knows they're happening.

At first, I used my empathy gift to understand, too, but it was painful and unproductive. I turned it off, and while I can imagine how everyone is feeling, at least I'm not experiencing it all the time. I hope Jax did the same.

Nic shakes his head, "No, we can't talk to her about this in public, and I doubt she'll willingly go with us somewhere private based on how she's feeling right now."

That's a valid point. We don't need to draw the humans' attention.

"So we just need to get past Anna and see her tonight," Jeremy says, starting to stand up again.

This time, Nic puts a hand on his shoulder and lightly pushes him back into his seat.

"We need a plan for getting past Anna first Jer. Sit tight."

"We could use magic," I hesitantly suggest. I hate suggesting it. It feels wrong to use magic on Anna. I know Aly wouldn't approve or appreciate it.

Jax shakes his head. "No, we can't, and I know you don't want to. Aly would be more upset about that than anything else that's happened."

I nod, a sense of relief filling me at the idea being shot down.

"Okay, maybe we can try to explain to Anna why we need to talk to Aly," Jay suggests.

"Yeah, that'll go well. Hey Anna, listen. I know this sounds crazy, but we told Aly we are magical and that she's forever bonded to Jeremy. We all want that with her, too, but for some reason, she ran off and is avoiding us. Can we please talk to her?" I respond in my most sarcastic voice.

"Okay, smart ass, why don't you suggest something then?" Jay responds, clearly agitated at his second idea being shot down so quickly. But I know I had a fair point.

"Rein it in. We are all on edge, but we need to work together, not be at each other's throats," Nic snaps at us.

We all lean back and try to appear relaxed at his command but I'm pretty sure none of us achieve it.

Jeremy looks up, his face lighting up with hope. "I think she's getting closer, she's furious, but I think she's coming here."

We all jump up at that. Jeremy is slower to get up like he's making sure she's really getting closer. But since he doesn't seem like he's about to bolt, I'm guessing she is.

"She could have gotten frustrated and wants answers," Jay suggests.

"Or the bond was pulling on her, and she finally gave in," Jeremy says, his eyes shining with hope.

"But she's mad, right? So be prepared for that," I remind everyone. This isn't about to be the sweet reunion we all want it to be. It's probably going to go horribly, but hopefully, we can get her the information she needs to make this better.

A hard knock at our door startles all of us, even though we are expecting her. We all freeze and turn toward the door, almost in slow motion.

I'm the first to break free and I realize I have a chance to set the mood of this visit for the better.

I open the door, and before she can get a word out, I wrap her up in a big hug, lifting her feet off the ground and spinning her around. "Aly! You're here. We've missed you so much!"

I set her down and she looks so thrown by my display. Mission achieved because it melted some of her anger.

Nine

Aly

Kiran is grinning at me like I just came by to hang out, and nothing could possibly be wrong. His smile is so big that it almost tempts me to smile back. Almost.

I turn away from him since it's harder to stay mad when he looks at me like that. Plus, it's not him I'm upset with.

I scan the room until my gaze stops on the object of my anger, Jeremy. He's just standing there, staring at me. He has no emotion on his face, and he doesn't acknowledge me or how angry I am.

I march right up to him and jab a finger in his chest.

"You!" I shout.

"Me?" He responds evenly and a little mockingly.

"What the hell is this?!" I ask, lifting my shirt to show the pentagram on my ribs. I swear I see him smile for a second, but then he's back to stone-faced.

"Are you happy about this?" I ask in response to the

millisecond of a smile I saw.

He smiles a little bigger. "Yeah, I am. It looks excellent there."

"Why the hell is it there?" I ask.

"Well, that's what we've been trying to get a hold of you to talk about. Are you finally ready to talk or are you going to keep pouting?" he responds.

I think I can feel steam shooting out of my ears, I'm so mad. How can he mock me right now? Hasn't he hurt me enough?

It's like he feels that momentary pang of hurt because his eyes show sympathy before switching back to empty.

I turn away from him, because he isn't going to tell me and land on Nic.

"What is going on, Nic?" I ask.

He steps forward and grabs my hand to start pulling me to the living room couch. I let him because I'm pretty sure I couldn't stop him if I tried.

"We have a lot to tell you, then you and Jeremy need to talk, really talk," he says pointedly to Jeremy, who appears a little sheepish at the chastising.

"Fine, start with the info, and we can go from there," I agree.

Nic stares at Jeremy, but when he doesn't say anything, he brings his attention back to me.

"That." Nic points to the spot where the new tattoo is, even though it's back under my shirt. "Is your mating mark from Jeremy."

"I'm marked?!" I say, outraged. It feels like I've been branded like cattle.

"Calm down, it's not like that. He has one, too, and it's a manifestation of your bond and the connection you share. It's a show of trust because that mark means a lot to Jeremy," Nic says with a pointed look and I calm down some at that explanation.

Aly

And I'm a little intrigued. What is my mark like? Why is that symbol important to him?

I start with the easier one. "Can I see it?"

Jeremy hesitates but after a fake cough from Kiran, he lifts his shirt. As he lifts it, I'm searching everywhere for something. I assume it's going to be over his ribs, but his tattoos are everywhere. How am I supposed to know which it is?

Then he lifts it over his chest, and I know right away what mark is mine. I hop up to inspect it closer. It's a deep red, like it was carved into his skin and then healed. It's a little eerie, but to me, it feels special. I have a connection to the mark. It calls to me.

I reach my hand out to touch it and barely make contact when Jeremy lets out a small grunt.

My eyes shoot up to his, and they are full of heat. If I had to describe them in one word, it would be smoldering. We continue staring into each other's eyes, and for a second, I think about acting on the impulses I'm feeling. The idea of kissing him or touching the mark again sounds brilliant, but a cough from behind me breaks the moment, and we jump apart like we've been burned.

I clear my throat. "So, what else do you need to tell me?"

They're all holding back laughs, but I won't hit them for it as long as I don't hear a chuckle.

"Well, you've probably been feeling the effects of the mate bond. We wanted to tell you so you knew what was happening. It's why we were harassing you so much," Jay says.

I feel a little bad that I've been ignoring them if they were just worried and trying to help.

"Okay, tell me now," I say instead of apologizing because I'm still feeling cranky about it all, even if guilt has now been added to the cocktail of emotions I'm feeling.

"It's hard for mates to be apart, especially right after mating. I'm sure you've been feeling itchy or a tug to go somewhere else. That's the mate bond trying to bring you back. If you were feeling it, I bet it has stopped now," Nic informs me. And he's right, any discomfort I was feeling has stopped.

"You can also get a sense of each other's emotions," Jay adds but I'm not sure about that one. I can think of once or twice I felt that way but not all the time.

Like Jeremy can sense my doubt, he says, "You won't have been feeling that one. I put a wall up to stop mine from leaking into you."

I should be grateful, that was considerate since I didn't know what was going on. Something I would not expect from him. But instead, I feel hurt and a little betrayed for some reason that he would do that.

I glimpse around the room, and the guys are glaring at Jeremy. I make a mental note to ask them why this feels bigger than it sounds. If my feelings are anything to go by, it is.

"As the bond grows," Nic pauses then corrects, "if the bond grows, things will feel more like a two-way street between each other, thoughts and emotions flowing freely in an intimate connection. Some mates are even able to communicate through their minds."

I can't imagine having an intimate connection with Jeremy, even if my mind and body crave it.

"Although, if you let us add you to the pack, you will automatically have a mind link with us all," Jay adds, hopeful.

"Pack?" I ask.

"That's not something you need to consider now if you don't want to. We can discuss that later," Nic says, giving Jay a pointed

Aly

look.

I'm intrigued, but my mind is currently full, and I'm having a hard enough time digesting everything else, so I decide to let that go for now. I pivot back to the topic at hand.

"So basically, I need to spend more time over here to avoid any issues with the bond?" I ask.

"Yes, and the more time you spend with Jeremy the quicker the bond will settle down. You will always crave each other's company and suffer if you're apart for too long," Nic answers.

I contemplate Jeremy, and I'm not sure what he sees on my face, but he stands up before addressing the room.

"Can you all give Aly and me a few to talk alone?"

I'm shocked he wants to but very interested in what he has to say. The guys all nod before making their way out of the room. Some of them give me a pat or a quick kiss on the head while they exit.

Ten

Aly

Once all the guys leave, Jeremy comes to sit next to me on the couch. He sits a respectful distance away, and I find myself wishing he had sat closer.

"What do you want to talk about?" I ask.

He doesn't say anything for a minute, staring at me before finally spitting out, "I'm not good at this."

What does that mean?

"Not good at what?" I say carefully.

"Communicating or expressing my emotions and, apparently, I've been doing an even worse job than usual."

I pause not knowing what to say but landing on, "Okay?"

He groans, throwing his hand up to cover his face and hide away from me.

"This is what I mean. I don't know how to have this conversation with you."

"And what conversation is that?" I ask gently, actually feeling

Aly

bad for him.

"I'm just going to spit it out. Aly, I want to be your mate. I want to do this right, and I'm hoping you'll give me a chance to do that."

Holy. Shit. Honestly, that was the last thing I had expected. I'm shocked into silence while he stares at me, waiting for an answer.

"Can you say something?" he asks.

"Honestly, I'm just shocked and trying to process. I thought you hated me…" I trail off, hoping he'll explain.

"I've never hated you, baby girl. I've been so drawn to you from the beginning. I decided a while ago that I wasn't going to have a mate. I had given up on that idea," he says painfully.

"Why?" I whisper, hoping he'll share this with me.

He hesitates, and I think he's not going to answer, but he surprises me by saying, "I got my heart broken by the girl I thought was going to be my mate one day."

My heart breaks for him, and I hate to say I feel jealous he had that connection with someone else.

He looks up from his lap sharply. "There's nothing to be jealous of, Aly. What I felt for her is nothing in comparison to what I feel for you, even before we've given this a chance."

My heart warms at that, and I feel infinitely better.

"So, can I ask what happened?" I ask hesitantly.

He nods. "Yes, but I want to be clear. It's a completely different situation than you. I can see that now." I nod, and he continues, "We were dating, and even though it's common for women to have multiple mates, she had always told me she only wanted me. She was a demon, and we weren't spending time with other demons, so I believed her."

I interrupt, "What does the demon thing have to do with it?"

He looks unsure but, again, surprises me by answering anyway, "It's not common for mates to be from multiple species. It's not impossible because we choose our mates when we don't find our fated, but it's so uncommon I didn't expect it."

"Expect what?" I ask.

"She... wanted the rest of the guys too. I didn't realize she was mostly using me as the opening for all of them. They were never big fans, so nothing happened, but when I realized, I was hurt. She told me she only wanted me, but that was a lie."

Oh no, so I'm exactly what he didn't want, someone he would have to share.

"Oh, Jeremy, I'm so sorry. You would absolutely be enough for anyone... I'm sorry I can't give that to you," I say sadly. Now I understand why he hated me. I am fated for all of his friends.

He leans forward, grabs my chin, and draws my gaze back to him.

"It's different with you, Aly, I didn't see it at first, but you weren't playing me or lying to me. You've always made your interest in all of us clear and I *want* to share you with my best friends. It will be hard sometimes, but it'll be worth it."

He says it so earnestly that I can't help but believe him. I give him a small smile and reach out to squeeze the hand that's not on my face. It slowly migrated from my chin to cupping my cheek.

"Okay," I whisper.

He actually smiles back at me, and it is the most gorgeous smile I've ever seen. He has dimples, and his eyes light up. It's incredible, and I want to see it again and again.

"So, in the name of trying to work this out, can I take you on a date?" He asks, kind of awkwardly, but it's sweet, and I eagerly nod my head yes.

Aly

I'm gifted with another smile that warms my heart.

He leans in, still cupping my cheek, and tentatively brushes his lips against mine. When I don't pull away, he crushes his lips to mine and immediately licks my lips, requesting entry.

When I open my mouth for him, our tongues tangle, and I can't help moaning into his mouth. He captures the moan and rewards me with a groan of his own. All too quick, he's pulling back but he drops another kiss on my lips before leaning back.

"Why is this symbol important to you?" I ask.

"Well, if someone has that symbol, they can summon me. It's a demon thing, but giving it to you as my mate mark is a sign of trust," he answers.

I give him a big smile. I like that. I am hopeful that we can make this a real mate bond, but I have one more question for him.

"Jer? Can I ask you another question?"

"Of course," he responds.

"Why does you blocking our bond feel like a big deal?"

His face drops, and he looks so guilty.

"Because it is, I'll stop right now, I'm sorry Aly. I did it to help you since you wouldn't know what you were feeling. I'm sure some strong emotions still made it through, but I wanted to make it easier on you. It's disrespectful to the bond for your mate to do it, and I could feel your hurt when I told you I had."

I want to be mad, but he did it for me and it would have been harder if he had let all his emotions through.

"But you'll take it down now?" I ask.

"Yes."

And I feel it all come rushing in. I can feel Jeremy as if he's a part of me. I can tell what he's feeling and it almost feels like I can reach out to him on the bond. I'm more complete, even though I didn't realize I was missing anything.

"Thank you," I whisper, and he drops another quick kiss on my lips, appearing happy himself.

Eleven

Aly

It's late, so we eventually split up for bed. I know I can't leave tonight. I need to be in the same place as Jeremy for a while.

I walk over to Nic, with a sweet smile on my face, and he gives me a cocky grin in return.

"Yes, you can stay with me. You don't even need to ask," he says.

He grabs my hand and tugs me upstairs until we reach his room, and then he shuts the door behind us.

"I missed you. I was worried not being able to get a hold of you, princess," he confesses.

I walk up to him and wrap my arms around his back. He follows suit.

"I know. I'm sorry, I won't cut you off like that again," I promise. He visibly deflates at that reassurance, and I feel even worse about putting him through that.

I lean up and give him a soft kiss as an apology. It quickly turns into a searing kiss that takes my breath away. From Nic's heavy breathing, I think it affects him just as much.

There's a knock at the door, which makes me jump, but Nic just chuckles.

"Want to guess which one of them it is?" Nic asks.

I assume they're here to sleep with Nic and me, so I immediately narrow it down to Kiran or Jay. Jeremy and I aren't there yet, and Ajax is way too shy.

Since Jay has done it before I go with him. "Jay."

Nic smiles and then pushes me towards the door to answer it, I guess that's his way of giving me the choice since this was heading towards more than sleep. I wouldn't mind Jay or Kiran joining in, the idea of them sharing me is seriously hot.

I open the door to see Jay there smiling down at me, but after one deep inhale, his eyes turn heated. Can he smell what we were just starting?

"Yes?" I ask sweetly.

"Don't tease Aly Kat. Can I join you, or will you send me away with a goodnight kiss?" he responds.

I lean up to kiss him, and he doesn't even look disappointed. I guess he really would be okay with just a goodnight kiss. Instead of stopping at his lips, I go up to his ear and whisper, "Come on in."

I back away from the door and right into Nic's hands, which he drops to my hips and uses to pull me tight against him.

Nic drops his mouth to my ear before whispering, "Well, this should be fun."

He starts dropping kisses along my neck as Jay steps up. He brings his hands right to my cheeks and comes in for a long, unhurried kiss. I try to get more from him but he's in complete control of the kiss, so I can only take what I'm given. I shift

Aly

back against Nic and feel his hard-on digging into me. I rub against him, and he bites my neck in return.

I'm surrounded by the two of them and it is such a turn-on. Two incredibly hot, muscular, amazing men want me, it's unreal.

Jay releases my mouth and starts kissing down the opposite side of my neck. When he gets to the top of my shirt, he grunts in annoyance before tugging on it.

"This has got to go, Aly Kat."

He steps back slightly, giving me room to take it off, but I want the same from them.

"Yours too then, both of you," I say, looking back at Nic.

I reach down and slip my shirt over my head, tossing it aside. Then I unbutton my pants before sliding them off as well. Luckily, I'm wearing a decent bra and underwear since I didn't get dressed with this in mind.

Before I can remove those, Jay's hands are back on me and I only get a second to browse his sexy physic. He has muscles on muscles, which are toned in every way. He stripped down to his boxers, but I can feel Nic still has his pants on behind me. His hands are hot against my skin as his mouth picks back up at my shoulder. He continues kissing down until he's sucking on my nipple through my bra.

I moan, arching my back, and Nic takes my jaw in his hand, guiding my mouth back to meet his lips. He claims my mouth, his lips caressing mine and parting my lips for him. His tongue meets mine, and I groan, which he captures in his mouth.

I can feel Nic's other hand trail up my spine until he finds my bra. He quickly unclasps it, causing it to fall forward. Jay tugs it off me immediately and starts in on my nipples, for real.

Nic's hand comes around and takes over, tweaking and

rolling my nipples while he is still kissing me. Jay takes that as his cue to move on and kisses down my stomach until he hits my panties.

This time, instead of kissing me over my underwear, he just rips them off my body and hands them up to Nic. Nic takes them, breaking the kiss and staring me in the eye as he puts them in his pocket before resuming kissing me.

Jay parts my legs more for him before running his finger up my leg and lightly across my pussy. I think he's going to play with me using that finger, but instead, it slips inside me just as his mouth seals over my clit. I moan out, and this time, Nic releases my lips so nothing suppresses the sound.

"Do you like that, princess? Having Jay go down on you?" he asks.

"Yes, so much," I say.

In response, Jay sucks harder and flicks his tongue across my clit as he sucks. I start shaking and putting more weight against Nic, to the point he's holding me up.

"Do you want him to make you come?" he asks.

"Yes, please!" I cry out, and Jay does just that. He sucks harder, adds another finger, and does the come here motion inside me. I shatter around him, screaming out, and Nic ends up completely holding my weight.

"Good girl, do you want more?" Nic whispers in my ear, running his fingers through my hair.

"Yes," I groan.

Jay stands up in front of us, and I can see my arousal glistening on his mouth still. Staring me dead in the eyes, he licks it off before coming to kiss me again. Jay picks me up by my thighs, and I feel his cock pressing into me through his boxers.

Aly

He tosses me onto the bed until I'm looking up at the both of them at the end of it. Nic moves, taking his pants and boxers off in one go before sitting on the bed with his back against the headboard. I don't need any further instruction. I straddle him rubbing my pussy against his long, hard length.

"Fuck, this is a great view," he says before lifting me and dropping me back down on top of him. I slide down until I meet his hips, the instant feeling of being so full making me groan as he rubs against all my nerve endings.

Nic's hands on my hip encourage me to move, bouncing up and down, with his help, on top of him. I brace my hands on his shoulder for leverage and lean in to kiss him as I move slowly and deliberately. As I pull back, Nic bites his lip before groaning himself and pulling me down, hard, on top of him, to a stop.

I gaze at him in question before he uses his strength to flip me over so I'm still straddling him, but this time I'm facing Jay. He does all this while keeping himself inside of me, and it's truly impressive.

I look up at Jay, who is kneeling before me, palming his cock and observing us over with so much heat in his eyes, it could start a fire.

"Open up, Aly Kat," Jay says, bringing his tip to my lips. I don't hesitate, opening up fully for him and sucking him down. He groans when I get him all the way in and swallow around his length. I lick around the head when I pull back, and he grabs my head, threading his fingers through my hair, and thrusts back in, deep.

Nic lifts me up slightly until he's thrusting into me again, and the double assault is amazing. Nic reaches around, rubbing my clit until I shatter around them. I can feel my pussy milking

Nic's cock until he comes. The moan vibrates around Jay until he shoots into the back of my throat, and I swallow every drop.

I collapse back onto Nic, and he catches me against him. He mumbles a spell into my hair, and suddenly, I'm clean again after everything we just did. He rolls me to the side so his front is pressed against my back. Jay hops into bed and brings us nose to nose as he snuggles in against me as well.

"That's a handy trick," I comment around a yawn. That took a lot out of me, and I'm about to crash.

"Yes, it is. Now, go to sleep, princess," he whispers.

Wrapped up between the two of them, I do just that.

Twelve

Aly

After spending the night at the guys' house, I really do feel better being closer to Jeremy. I slept incredibly, wrapped in Nic and Jay's arms, and it was nice just to be back together with them.

I wake up in Nic's bed, expecting to be surrounded by their warmth but both sides of the bed are empty. I lift my head off the pillow and search his room but there's no sign of either of them.

When I get up, I don't have anything on. I wasn't planning on spending the night when I came over here, furious, so I didn't bring any clothes with me.

I don't want to put jeans on when I'm just lounging around their house so I sneak a peak in Nic's drawers for a pair of sweatpants and a t-shirt. Everything in there is meticulously folded. I'm afraid to mess anything up. I grab the sweatpants sitting on top and try not to disturb anything else. The next drawer has t-shirts, so I carefully grab one of those, too. A small part of me wants to ruffle the entire drawer, just to make him mad, but I decide to save that urge for another time.

Pulling on his sweatpants, I take a quick stop in the bathroom attached to his room. I do my business and try to make myself more presentable. Again, everything in his bathroom is perfect, so it's easy to find what I need, but he will know I was in here. I wonder what he would do if I used his toothbrush.

Instead of risking his wrath, I put some toothpaste on my finger and rub it around, then use his comb to help my hair. I look ten percent better but I shrug my shoulders and head out, it'll have to be enough.

I hear voices coming from the kitchen so I start heading that way. It sounds like they're all there, and I take a moment to just listen to them joking around and happy. It sounds like Jay was trying to make eggs and somehow Kiran got in his way. They sound so light and happy, I love getting to hear them this way.

I step into the kitchen, and all eyes turn to me. I start with Nic to see if he's mad about the clothes, but his eyes are heated as he scans me, so I think I'm safe.

He gets up from the table and gives me a quick kiss before whispering in my ear, "I like you in my clothes."

I get a shiver down my spine at the possessiveness in that statement. I give him a wink and a small smile, trying not to let it show how hot that makes me feel. I think I fail.

Kiran comes over next with a mug of coffee. "Here, baby, dark with nothing in it, just like you like it."

And he's right, that is just how I like it, and I feel so special he's paid attention to that.

"Do you want some eggs, Aly Kat?" Jay asks from in front of the stove.

Aly

"That would be great, thanks, Jay."

I head towards the table, and before I can decide where to sit, Jeremy surprises me by pushing out the chair next to him with his foot and making eye contact. His face doesn't convey anything, but I can feel hopefulness through the bond.

I decide to go along with it. We are trying after all and I'm craving some closeness with him too.

Once I sit down, Jax speaks up from across the table, "How'd you sleep Aly?"

"Good, thanks. I'm a lot better than I have been now that I'm here," I say, giving Jeremy a guilty look.

He nods in understanding, and it hits me for the first time that he was suffering just like me. Any effects I was feeling, he was possibly feeling double since I wasn't shielding him at all.

I grab his hand and lean in closer, so it's just between us. "I'm sorry I put you through that, I didn't know."

He gives me a nod and a small smile. "It's okay, you didn't know. We will figure it out now."

I may not be able to read him, but I have a direct connection to his feelings now, and it's so clear to me how much he feels under that shell. He's excited, I'm guessing, for us to figure things out, and he's content, maybe because I'm here. I would have never known if I didn't feel it myself.

I squeeze his hand and turn back to the room. They're all watching our interaction, and their faces clearly show they're happy about it. How did they hear what I said?

Then it hits me, I know they're supernatural but I don't know what that means or what they can do.

"Can you guys tell me more about each of your abilities and what being each of your species means?" I ask.

They all look a little shocked and happy, and it's probably

because I'm showing interest.

"Of course we can! Let's have breakfast first, then we can go over it all later," Nic responds for the group, and they all nod their agreement, including me.

Jay comes over with a plate of eggs and a side of bacon and toast, which he sets in front of me. When he leans in to set it down, he nuzzles into my neck, making me laugh and push him away. He seems pretty content when I turn to thank him.

"Thank you! Have you always known how to cook, Jay?"

His smile gets bigger. "Yeah, I really enjoy cooking. This is nothing. You've got to let me make you a big, outrageous meal sometime."

I smile back. "That sounds great!"

"Soon?" he asks hopefully, and I find myself agreeing right away.

"Soon sounds great."

He drops a kiss on my lips before walking back to the counter to finish serving up some plates.

The best part is that I didn't feel any jealousy through my bond with Jeremy and that settles something in me.

The guys all grab their plates, and we settle in around the table for breakfast.

"Shoot, is today Monday?" I ask.

Jax smothers a laugh. "Yes, it is, but don't worry. Our class got canceled today. I guess the professor is sick. We would have woken you if you slept too long, and we still had class."

My adrenaline settles down, and I can't believe I forgot to set an alarm. That's really unlike me, but I guess I've had a lot on my mind.

"We still have math later, though," Kiran complains, and I pat his hand with sympathy.

Aly

"We can all go together. It'll be great," Jay adds.

We all dig into our food and eat with gusto. Even if it was a simple meal, Jay did an incredible job. I really will have to take him up on his offer for an outrageous meal.

Just when we are finishing up, and I'm about to demand we talk about their powers, my phone starts ringing. I pull it out to see I have a couple of missed calls and texts from Anna. My stomach sinks, I didn't tell her I was leaving, let alone that I would be gone all night.

"It's Anna, I've got to take this," I say, hopping up and leaving the room while hitting accept.

"Anna, I'm so sorry!" I say before she can dig into me.

"Aly! You had me so worried. Where are you?" she shouts back.

"I'm... at the guys' house," I hesitate because I don't know how she will feel about that.

"You made up with them?" she asks.

"Yes," I respond slowly.

She lets out a sigh. "Thank goodness! I was really worried and they clearly care about you so much. Since I'm so happy you made up, I won't be mad, but you owe me for making me worry!"

"You're the best. I will make it up, I swear! I, unfortunately, have one more request."

"If it's to take care of Bailey, I already did. No worries, girl," she responds, reading my mind.

"Thank you so much! I will pick him up later and bring him here since I may be staying over for a few days."

"Okay, go enjoy your man meat, and let's talk later!" she says and we hang up.

I can't believe I forgot to tell her. Even with everything I have going on, she's my best friend, and I need to do better. Now, it's time to get some answers about these guys.

Thirteen

Aly

I head back into the kitchen to see the guys have already cleaned up after breakfast.

"Everything okay with Anna?" Jax asks when he sees me enter.

"Yes, I forgot to tell her where I was or that I was sleeping here. She was worried."

Nic walks up and cups my cheek, "I'm sorry she was worried but I'm glad you have such a great friend watching out for you."

I can feel myself blush under his attention, and he's right. Anna is a fantastic friend.

"Can I learn more about you guys before we need to go to class?" I ask, changing the subject.

"Sure, go get settled in the living room, and we will join you in a minute." He turns around and looks at Jeremy. "Jer go join her and get some skin-to-skin contact in since you guys will be in public later."

Jeremy gives him a nod and then gets up to come join me. When we get to the couch, I stand there awkwardly, but Jeremy takes charge, sitting down and pulling me into his lap.

"I've wanted to have you in my lap since I saw you in Ajax's," he whispers in my ear and I shiver.

"You wanted me then?" I ask, turning to look at him.

"I've wanted you since you fell in my lap at the bar," he confesses.

I smile and lean in to kiss him.

"Why do we need contact since we will be around people?" I ask, unsure why Nic said that.

He sighs. "Well, it's going to be hard for both of us to be surrounded by people we may see as competition. I'm not sure how you will handle it since I don't know what you are, but I'm going to want to beat every guy who comes near you to a pulp. Some contact now will help the bond settle and calm those instincts down."

I nod even though I don't fully understand the instincts part. The guys keep talking about the instincts of their species. Hopefully, it's something this conversation helps clear up.

I can feel the bond singing at the contact between Jeremy and me, and I never want it to stop. It's incredible.

The rest of the guys come join us, taking up spots around the rest of the room, and something occurs to me.

I turn to Jeremy. "Do you feel that way with them?"

He shakes his head. "No, the bond must know they're fated for you, too, because I feel completely comfortable with them around you. Better even because you're well protected."

Ever since we talked yesterday, Jeremy has seemed more talkative when I ask him questions. I like hearing what he's thinking.

Aly

"So, where should we start?" I ask the room.

Jay raises his hand like we are in school, and I point to him.

"Well, I think mine may be the simplest, so let's start there. Sound good?"

"Yes," I respond.

"So, I'm a wolf shifter, which means I turn into a wolf. I share the same instincts a wolf has, like to surround my mate with my scent or a stronger sense to protect her. I'm very territorial, although you're the exception to that because I want you covered in my scent and surrounded by my things. I also want to wear your scent so other females know I'm taken. It's all very primitive, but I share my soul with a wolf, so," he finishes shrugging his shoulders.

A lot more makes sense with that explanation. Especially why he's always nuzzling me.

"That... explains a lot," I say, "can I see your wolf?"

Jay seems excited and stands up right away. He starts stripping off his clothes, and I raise an eyebrow in question.

"I would destroy the clothes if I shifted in them," he explains.

And before my eyes, Jay's body transforms into a giant wolf. He's grey with black mixed in, and he's as tall as I am when I stand up.

He steps hesitantly closer to me, and I lift my hand in the air to give him the choice whether I can touch him or not. He bounds forward, nuzzles against my neck like Jay always does, and gives my face a big lick.

"Oh, Jay!" I admonish.

I pet him and run my fingers through his fur. His tongue pops out, and his tail starts wagging, making him seem like an overgrown dog.

I make the mistake of saying so, and he gives me an annoyed

glare, but as a wolf, it's still cute. I keep that to myself.

Jeremy must think we've had enough because he reaches forward and pulls me back down into his lap.

Jay clearly doesn't want to lose my attention because he hops up next to me on the couch.

Nic stops him. "Jay, you'll destroy the couch. Come on!"

Jay's wolf gives Nic a glare, but he hops down to the floor. He takes a seat right by my legs and rests his head in my lap. He gives me sweet eyes, and I pet him, making his tail wag again.

This reminds me that I need to ask the guys if I can bring Bailey here.

"Hey, before we continue, could I bring Bailey over for a couple days while I'm staying here? I don't want to push him off on Anna and I don't like being apart from him."

Instead of the response I'm expecting, a 'for sure' or 'sorry no', they all look around at each other. I can't interpret their faces. Jeremy is feeling unsure and a little guilty, as well.

"What's going on?" I ask them.

"Well, Bailey isn't a normal dog. We aren't sure what he is, but he's clearly magical and from our world," Nic reveals.

Oh shit, are they serious? How can that be true? They must see the mystified look on my face because Jax continues.

"We will add investigating what Bailey is to our research about what you are, maybe they're connected."

"He seems familiar to me but I can't place where," Kiran adds.

"Okay, that all sounds good, still, can I bring him? Magical or not, I love him and feel connected to him," I say.

"Of course, we just thought you should know," Nic says.

I nod, setting that aside to deal with later. Right now, I want to focus on learning more about the guys.

"Who is next?" I ask.

Aly

Nic volunteers. "I'm a mage, which is something I'm sure you've seen in media, but you can't go based on that. I can cast spells or sometimes use concentrated magic to make things happen. If a spell is too much for me, I can use powerful objects or things to enhance my powers, like Jeremy's blood."

I nod, acknowledging what he had to do to save me when the memory spell was too much.

"I'm not naturally gifted with things like enhanced hearing like they are, but every morning I cast a few spells to magnify my senses. It helps me be more on top of things. You can use spells for almost anything it's just a matter of how powerful you need to be."

"Can I see some?" I ask.

"Sure," he says. Then he lifts his hands and makes a small motion, muttering something, and a ball of light forms in his palm. It's beautiful and otherworldly, and it's just a ball of light. What would seeing something more complex be like?

"Have you ever used magic on me besides the memory spell?" I ask.

Nic is sheepish and a little guilty. "Well, when that guy hugged you in front of us, we all went a little crazy. You have to understand that supernaturals have crazy instincts in general, but especially when it comes to their mate. We are all territorial and want to protect you, just not as extreme as Jay," he says.

Jeremy tightens his arms around me at the reminder. Jay nudges my hand, clearly wanting me to resume petting him. I oblige but bring my attention back to Nic.

"So what did you do?" I ask.

"I gave you a stronger-than-usual static shock so he would let you go. I imagine you don't remember it because of the spell," Nic says, and he's right; I don't.

I have a million more questions, but first, I want to learn the basics about all of them.

"Hey guys, I hate to cut this short but we need to leave for class unless we are skipping?" Kiran asks hopefully.

I don't want us to all miss class, and I especially don't want to. This can wait.

"No, we are going. Will you tell me the rest after?" I ask and they all confirm they will.

I hurry up and get dressed for the day, and the guys are already ready, so we head out.

Fourteen

Ajax

"I call sitting next to Aly!" Jay says as we walk across campus to get to class. I'm standing next to Nic, and I see him roll his eyes at Jay's antics. I'm not going to step in though, I know Aly doesn't like having to choose who she sits next to. This saves her from that, and that makes me happy. Plus, I usually have a class alone with her before this so as far as I'm concerned, I'm already winning.

"Fine, but we better let Jeremy have her other side, or the math class might see a real-life demon for the first time," Nic says.

I turn towards Jeremy who is standing very close to Aly and watching everyone who walks past us. So far, I don't think Aly has felt the instinct to protect their bond that we warned her of, but he does. He's agitated, clenching and unclenching his fists as he glares at anyone who dares to get too close.

"What do you look like in your demon form?" She asks him,

I'm guessing trying to distract him from his glaring but also out of curiosity. I'm sure she will want to see all of our forms now that she saw Jay's wolf.

"I'll show you sometime," he answers distractedly and without taking his eyes off our surroundings. Being around all these people has him worked up. If it keeps going like this, I have a feeling class will go terribly.

She turns to Nic. "When will our bond settle down?"

"Well, it depends on the couple and how long it takes them to form a solid relationship. Since you and Jeremy didn't have a relationship before the bond formed, I think it's going to take a lot longer," he answers.

"But, if you were to mate with someone you had a stronger connection with, it would take less time for the bond to settle down," Jay adds eagerly, probably thinking about himself.

We make it to class and Aly takes her usual seat in the middle, with Jeremy on one side and Jay on the other. Kiran and I sit next to Jay, and Nic sits next to Jeremy. Hopefully, being so surrounded will help Jeremy calm down. I feel bad for him. This seems more intense than usual. I wonder if it's more intense because they are fated mates, not just chosen mates.

A few people wave over at us as they pass, which isn't unusual. Even if they aren't waving at Aly, Jeremy growls a little under his breath. One glance at Jeremy right now, and anyone would go running, even in his completely human form. Not that he is usually friendly, but now he's downright hostile.

I pull my laptop out and open what I need for class, completely ignoring my surroundings. Which is how I don't realize that mean girl from the library is coming this way until she's stopped right in front of Jeremy. What's her name again? The incident in the library was a close call. We heard what was going on with our enhanced hearing, and Aly was confused about how we had stepped in so quickly. I was confused as to why she didn't question us further, but now I guess we know it was the memory spell.

I immediately tune into my empathy gift to check on Aly, and before the girl even opens her mouth, something in her snaps, and a hot rage surges through her system. I can feel her need to fight and cause pain. The current violence in her is unlike anything I've felt with her before. I hear a soft snap and see the pen in Aly's fingers snap, causing her hand to be covered in ink, but I don't think she notices. She certainly doesn't look down. She's too busy glaring death at that girl.

Aly clearly feels the need to protect her bond with Jeremy. Why did this girl have to pick today to challenge Aly again and approach one of us? And why in the world did she have to approach Jeremy?

The girl, of course, notices the ink, giving Aly a sly face. "Should you go get cleaned up, Aly? I can keep your friends entertained while you're gone."

I send a message down our pack bond, *"someone needs to do something before Aly loses it. We have no idea how she's going to react."*

Nic responds, *"I'm too busy trying to keep Jeremy calm. Aly's rage is feeding into him."*

Aly doesn't take the bait, but I can audibly hear her grinding her teeth.

The girl just rolls her eyes at Aly and then turns back to Jeremy. With a sickly sweet and so very fake voice, she says, "So I was wondering if you would want to hang out sometime? We could study for this class."

Aly is out of her seat unnaturally fast and in front of the girl.

She grips her arm and bends it at an unnatural angle. It looks like she's about to break it but hasn't pushed it quite that hard. How did she know when to stop before breaking it? Either way, if the girl says anything else, I'm sure we will have a broken arm to deal with.

Kiran, Jay, and I hop up and try to stop this from getting any worse. We are in class surrounded by humans. Aly can't do anything crazy that draws more attention to us.

I grab Aly's arm and turn her towards me, but her eyes are unfocused, and she keeps peering back at the girl like she's prey.

"Hey Aly, it's okay, look at me," I say while pumping soothing energy into her system. It's one of my powers as a light fae, and I use it to my advantage now. Her eyes slowly start to clear until I think she can see me again.

"Jax? What happened?" she asks before slumping a little into my arms. I catch her and bring her over to the nearest seat. She collapses into it immediately, drained from the incident.

I look up to see that Jay and Kiran have gotten the girl to leave, and Jeremy is focused on Nic.

"Something supernatural. I'll explain after class, okay?" I whisper.

She nods and then holds a hand up to her head in pain. Luckily, it's not the hand covered in ink. I pull out a tissue and start wiping that hand off. I'm about to ask Nic to heal her when I glance over and realize he's pale and weak, too.

"What happened to Nic while I was calming Aly down?" I ask down our bond.

"He cast a confusion spell over the whole class, which wiped him out, but he says we need to stay through class otherwise we will redraw attention to ourselves," Jay replies.

Ajax

"Pass me Aly's stuff," I say, and when Jay does, I help her get set up between Kiran and me. We don't want to get up and play musical chairs, so we all sit where we left off. There's a risk Jeremy could get worked up, but I imagine his instincts have calmed down since Aly defended their bond so strongly. It probably just strengthened some from that display, which will be reassuring to both of them.

Fifteen

Aly

We finish up class and I don't absorb anything the professor says. Hopefully, Jax was able to pay attention and can catch me up later. I feel really out of it after what I'm calling my incident. I think I finally understand what the guys mean when they say their instincts take over. I didn't feel like I had any control over myself when Kate came to talk to Jeremy. My instincts were screaming to neutralize the threat, and my body acted without my direction. When I remember it, it's through a haze, like I wasn't the one in control. I think I would have broken her arm or worse, and the crazy thing is, I think I knew how to do it.

We are all wiped, especially Nic and me, so we decide it's best to just head back to the house instead of the library, like usual. We need to get away from people so nothing else happens. This bond needs to settle down and fast; we can't keep living like this. I message Anna asking her to take care of Bailey again so we can go straight back to the house, and she quickly agrees.

Aly

We all start walking back, and I land myself next to Ajax. Of course, Jeremy is on my other side. He hasn't left it since class ended. After the incident was over, I could feel happiness and contentment mixed with his worry. It felt satisfying to him that I protected our bond so fiercely, even if he was worried about Nic and me.

"Jax, are you okay if we plan to work on the assignment tonight still? At the house?" I ask him. We have a weekly assignment for the computer science class we share. We were paired up and always met after this class at the library to work on the assignment. The rest of the guys usually tag along, but Jax and I do need that time.

"Yes, of course. Now that you're going to be spending more time at the house with all of us, we will probably work on our assignments more casually. Tonight sounds great, though." He reaches over and gives my hand a light squeeze. He goes to pull it away just as fast, but I hold on tight. He looks at me in shock but I just smile back and continue holding his hand.

I'm glad we have a class together. I don't want to lose that time with Ajax. It's important to have some scheduled one-on-one time with the shyest of my mates. It's crazy I'm already referring to them as my mates when I just found out, but it feels right.

When we get back to the house, Jeremy gives Nic some of his blood, something I should be grossed out by, but for some reason, I'm not. With all the craziness around me, I must be adjusting quickly.

Once Nic looks better, he comes to heal me, and we all settle in around the living room.

"So, what happened? Kate came up to Jeremy, and I lost it. Was that my supernatural side?" I ask.

"Yes, and a completely normal reaction. You shouldn't feel bad about it. We just need to work on some control. We can focus on it when we train," Nic answers.

"Jax, how did you get me to calm down?" I ask, one second I was furious and the next I was unnaturally calm.

"Well, that's one of my powers. Maybe we should continue the conversation from earlier? I can go next." Jax smiles at me.

I nod my head, eager to hear about what Jax can do.

"As a light fae, I need to gain power by absorbing happy emotions. I can't do as much unless I have power in my well. When I do, I can sense other people's emotions and make them feel certain positive emotions, like calm. I can also manipulate light to my will as a form of defense or even offense, but it's stronger as a defense."

So he filled me with calmness when I was freaking out about Kate, interesting.

"That's remarkable, Jax, thanks for telling me."

The logical next choice is Kiran, since his powers will probably be similar to his twin but he turns away and instead, Jeremy starts.

"Well, as you know, I am a demon. My blood is powerful and has healing properties. I have some magic, but it's not like Nic's."

That's all he says, not explaining any further. I roll my eyes at him but let it slide for now. I'm sure I can convince him to show me sometime. Words aren't his strong suit, but actions are.

I gaze at Kiran, and he's glum, which is not an expression I'm used to seeing on him.

"What is it, Kiran? Do you not want to tell me?" I ask, concerned.

Aly

"Dark fae don't have the best reputation, Aly. I don't want you to think differently about me," he confesses.

"I would never! Kiran, I know you, and what you are won't change that, I promise."

He nods. "Okay, well, it's very similar to Jax but the opposite. Instead of getting power from positive emotions, I get them from negative and instead of being able to cause positive emotions, I cause negative."

He looks away, not giving me a chance to show him I'm okay with that.

"So? Your powers are opposite." I get up and go sit on Kiran's lap. His arms automatically go around me, but I have to turn his head towards me to make eye contact. "It changes nothing. I think it's cool. I want you to show me sometime, okay?"

He picks up a little, his shoulders dropping and his arms feeling less stiff around me.

"I think that's enough for now. I'm sure I'll learn more just by being around you guys," I tell the group. This gave me enough of an idea for now, but I want to see them all in action. I've already gotten to see Jay and Nic, which helped me understand their powers more quickly. I have a feeling it will take a lot of coaxing to get Kiran to show me his.

They all nod, so I ask Jax, "Should we go work on our project?"

"Yeah, let's do it," he says, standing up. He reaches out and helps me out of Kiran's lap, and we head up to his room.

Sixteen

Aly

I'm thrilled to get some alone time with Jax. With everything going on it's been hard to come by.

We are set up in his room to work on our assignment. I'm excited to be in a more personal setting with him. I wondered if he would choose the kitchen over his room, but he led me here.

I like being in Jax's room, it reflects him. There are computers and monitors everywhere. It's a tech nerd's dream, so I'm incredibly jealous. The rest of his space is pretty bare. Clearly, he spent the most time on his technology setup.

He creates an excellent workspace for us, and we settle in with our books and computers surrounding us.

We get right to work on our project, and as always, Jax is incredible. He always knows what he's doing and can solve any problems I have. It's incredible that he already knows all of this. I wonder why he does.

Aly

"How did you get into code?" I ask. "Clearly you've been doing it for a while."

"Well, I've always been inquisitive and when I read a book about it, I got invested. I started reading more and working with the code. It made a lot of sense to me so I kept going until I was completely invested," he explains.

"Why take this class then?" I ask.

"Well, I want the degree, and to get that, I have to take the class. Plus, I can't help but feel like it's fate since I have it with you," he says.

I blush but go back to how he knows so much. He needs to know how amazing that is.

"That's incredible. You know I love how smart you are, right Jax?" I ask.

He ducks his head. "Really? You don't think it's nerdy?"

"Not at all Jax. I think it's hot. I… think you're hot, I'm really into you," I confess.

"Can we talk about you and me?" Jax asks.

"Of course, what do you want to talk about?"

"Well, I know you know I'm," he pauses before continuing, "a virgin."

I smile. "Yes, I do, Jax, and I love it. Honestly, you make me feel so special."

"I always want to make you feel special, Aly. To do that, I want to take things slow with you. I've always believed I would find my mate, and I want to do things right now that we have. Let's grow a connection together, and let me woo you a little. We don't need to rush anything. Are you okay with that?"

My heart melts. I love that the guys are all different, but I am especially grateful for how sweet and considerate Jax is. He wants us to build our bond, and I'm excited to do that, considering how my first bond went.

"Ajax, that sounds incredible. I love that, thank you."

I lean in close for a kiss, without actually touching his lips, giving him the option of kissing me or not. It seems like an exceptional first step.

He bridges the gap, tentatively touching his lips to mine but smoothly taking control without being controlling. He's not aggressive or demanding, but he still takes the lead and sets a rhythm for us.

The kiss is over too soon, but now that we've had our first kiss, I plan on having more and more often.

I give him a beaming smile so he knows how happy this has made me, and he smiles back.

It's crazy how opposite he is to his twin, but I love that they have their own personalities. They are completely their own people, even if they look identical.

"So should we get back to our project?" he asks.

"Or we could keep kissing," I suggest with a wink.

He leans in right away, and we do just that. We start slow until we are making out. His hand is tangled in my hair, and I climb on his lap. He runs his fingers firmly down my spine, and I shiver in his arms.

He brings his lips to my neck, feathering a soft kiss before surprising me and following it up with a hard nip. He licks up my neck before kissing down it again, and I feel my skin pebble under him.

"Aly," he groans when I grind down onto his hard-on.

"What? We still have all our clothes on," I point out, wiggling again.

He must agree because he brings one hand down to my hip and grinds me against him again harder. His tongue flicks

Aly

across my pulse point, and I moan.

I tangle my hand in his hair, tugging at it as I bring his lips back up to mine. I want him so bad, but I also love having this more innocent make-out and knowing it's not going anywhere else. It's surprisingly sexy, probably because it's with Ajax. I run my hand under his shirt, caressing his soft skin and feeling his muscles. He is as ripped as the rest of his friends. Is it a supernatural thing?

Eventually, I pull back and reluctantly remove myself from his lap. I drop one more quick kiss on his lips.

"Okay, now we should work," I say.

"Sure, because it'll be so easy to focus now," Jax jokes and punctuates it with a wink.

I laugh. "I love it when you joke with me. You're funny, Jax," I confess. Sometimes with Ajax, I feel like I get to share things that just come obviously to the other guys.

He beams at me, and I'm glad I said it.

"Good Aly, I always want to see you smiling, especially when it's directed at me."

I give him another smile just for that and turn back to my book with a blush staining my cheeks. I've never blushed as much in my life as I do around Jax.

We eventually finish our assignment, but we take a lot of breaks along the way, and I have no complaints.

Seventeen

Jay

I'm in the kitchen cooking a fancier dinner than usual to impress Aly. She complimented me on my cooking at breakfast, and I've spent all day thinking about what I should make her. I have a list a mile long, but tonight, I'm making homemade gnocchi. I've perfected my recipe over the years, and I want this dinner to be perfect. I love to cook, and I want to do that for my mate. Last night with her was incredible, and I want things to keep going that well.

I've already made the gnocchi, so before I boil it, I'm working on a homemade marinara sauce to accompany it. After finely chopping the garlic, all I need to do is cook it.

I don't want to interrupt Jax's time with her, but I also want to get the timing right, so I check in via the pack bond.

"Hey, how long until you guys are ready for dinner?"

There is a pause before Jax eventually answers, *"We can come down in ten minutes, does that work?"*

Jay

I respond, "Yes," and finish the sauce up before putting the gnocchi in to boil. When it floats to the top I pull it out, dishing it out for everyone as I go. The timer goes off and I pull out the garlic bread too. I know it smells incredible in here and I can't wait for Aly to come down and see it all.

The ten minutes goes fast and I'm just putting the finishing touches on when everyone comes in. The guys all give me appreciative nods but I'm not paying attention, I want to see Aly's reaction.

When she walks in, her eyes go wide, and she takes a big sniff before coming over to me and giving me a giant hug.

I can smell lust and Jax all over her, they must have been up to a little more than studying up there. Good for Jax. I'm sure they're going to take things slow, but I'm glad it's not no movement at all. I get harder smelling the lust all over her. Down, boy, that's not what this is about.

"Jay, did you do all this by yourself?" she asks.

"Yes, I did. It's homemade gnocchi, Aly Kat. I hope you like it," I say back, trying not to sound too excited or desperate.

She surprises me by hitting my arm softly before saying, "You don't have to do it all by yourself! I'm a terrible cook, but I'll help you."

I'm about to immediately deny that offer as I would with the guys, but then I realize this is a chance to spend more time with Aly. So instead, I accept. Even if she is a terrible cook, I'll teach her and it can be our thing together.

"That would be great, I'll let you know," I say, leaning in and giving her a soft kiss.

I can smell the shock coming off the guys that I accepted, but I want time with my girl. Even if that means sharing my kitchen. I'm territorial with them, but never with her. I want her in my space. Speaking of. "Hey, will you spend the night with me tonight?" I ask.

She beams up at me. "Sure, Jay, that sounds great."

I lean in and give her another kiss, this time taking my time more and enjoying it. The feeling of her lips against mine is heaven.

Before I can take it too far, Jeremy shouts from behind me, "The food is going to get cold!"

Even though he has a mating bond with her already, I know he's jealous. They're working on it, but their relationship isn't comfortable yet.

I pull back, smiling down at her, and she gives me one right back. We both ignore Jeremy but we do carry the food over to the table. Aly helps me and it feels amazing to do something so mundane, all together.

Everyone digs in, and it feels incredible when Aly goes on and on about how delicious the food is. I savor the taste but I'm already planning on getting to taste something better tonight.

I'm going to have Aly to myself tonight, in my room, in my bed, surrounded by my scent. I can feel my hard-on grow and stretch the boundaries of these pants.

Before I can continue fantasizing about Aly at the dinner table, Nic speaks up.

"I was thinking we could start looking into what you could be soon, Aly."

She smiles at him, but it's a little dim. "That sounds good, thanks. It's weird not knowing what you are. Do you think there's a chance I could accidentally do something or hurt someone?"

My heart hurts for her, it's hard enough when you have powers and can't control them. I tore through a million pants

Jay

with accidental shifts before I got control. To not have any idea what those powers could be must be even scarier.

"They've never emerged before, so there's no reason to believe they will now. I wouldn't stress about that," Jax says from across the table.

"That's true, although does today with Kate count?" she asks.

I barely restrain my growl over what happened with Kate. Someone threatening my mate, even if it's just a human, doesn't sit right with me or my wolf. I want the threat gone, but I know there's nothing I can do. It's not a real or physical threat to Aly.

"I don't think you did anything magical. You just confronted her, nothing obviously supernatural at least," Nic says.

"Okay, that's good." Aly's shoulders drop, and she sits back. I can't smell anxiety pouring off her anymore.

"Should we spend some time on it after dinner?" I suggest.

Everyone agrees, and even though that will delay my time with Aly, I'm hopeful we will find something. I don't like her anxiety, and I want it eased. Although, depending on what we find it could get worse.

Either way, I'll be there to support her.

Eighteen

Aly

———

We don't find anything and eventually decide to call it a night. I'm disappointed but the guys reassure me there's more to search through and that we won't stop looking. Jay immediately grabs my hand to drag me upstairs and we settle in on his bed.

He playfully tackles me to the mattress and I laugh, my remaining anxiety melting away. He runs his nose up my neck, leaving playful nips which turn me on more than make me want to play back. But instead of going in for the kiss, I surprise him by flipping us over, so I'm on top. I sit up, with my thighs bracketing him, and start tickling his sides.

He is very ticklish. He starts squirming all around, laughing and throwing some playful growls at me. The growls are clearly from his wolf and the sound turns me on.

"Mercy!" He finally shouts, and I grant it to him, stopping my assault.

Aly

We are both laughing when he leans up to kiss me before dropping back down to the bed.

"You are so incredibly gorgeous, especially when you're happy," he says, staring me straight in the eyes so I can see how much he means that.

"You're pretty gorgeous yourself," I respond, leaning in to kiss him again.

I slowly move my hips up and down against him. I can feel how hard he is against me already.

His hands come up and firmly grip my ass. He squeezes it before helping guide my motion against him.

I angle my head better so I can use my tongue. Tangling it with his and increasing my pace against him.

I break the kiss and lean up. Gripping the bottom of my shirt, I bring it over my head before tossing it to the side.

Jay groans, "Fuck you're gorgeous."

I smile down at him as I reach behind me, to flick my bra off.

"How about now?" I ask in what I hope is a flirty voice.

"Even better," he replies in an almost pained tone.

Jay leans up and sucks one of my nipples into his mouth. His hand comes up to play with the other. He's sucking, biting, twisting, and licking them, and it feels so damn satisfying.

"Jay," I moan, grabbing his head and holding him against my chest.

Eventually, though, I want more.

"More Jay, please!"

He breaks from my chest and gazes up at me with the sexiest damn smirk on his face.

"Anything for you, Aly Kat," he responds before quickly flipping us over, so he's on top.

As he settles above me, he ogles me from top to bottom, and

I feel like prey below him. He is all wolf right now.

Jay goes for my leggings, pulling them down my legs until I'm only left in my panties.

He leans up to take his shirt off, reaching behind his head to pull it off in a very hot way.

Coming back down, he brings his mouth close to my panties before looking up at me playfully. He grabs onto my underwear with his teeth and slowly pulls it down my legs before tossing it away.

When he stands up, he never takes his eyes off me as he removes his pants and boxers.

"I can smell how ready you are for me. Do you want this, Aly?" he asks.

I nod enthusiastically, but I think he wants words, too.

"Yes, so bad, Jay."

He lines up with my slit, rubbing his tip against me. Jay bumps it into my clit a few times, making me more desperate. He must see that desperation on my face because he finally guides himself in, but he stops after just the tip.

"Jay!" I groan, and he peers down at me playfully.

"Yes, Aly Kat?" he asks.

"I want more," he moves in another inch, "I want all of you," I clarify.

He moves in another inch.

"I'm savoring this, I want to remember the way you felt this first time, forever," he responds.

He gives me another inch, and I buck up, trying to get more.

"So impatient, okay, I'll give you what you want."

Then he plunges the rest of the way into me, and I cry out. He starts pumping into me hard and fast. I reach up to grab his shoulders, and I can feel my nails digging into his skin.

Aly

He's pounding into the bundle of nerves inside me, and it feels so damn incredible.

"Jay," I groan, "I'm so close."

"I know, give it to me. I want to feel you squeezing my cock, babe," he demands.

I come around him and it feels like bliss spreads all through my body. I lose conscious control of what I'm doing, but I feel myself rake my nails down his back.

"Fuck yes, Aly, mark me up," he groans, but he doesn't come too.

He slows his pace, working me through the last of my orgasm before continuing at a slower, softer pace.

"You are so damn sexy when you come for me," he whispers in my ear before nipping lightly at my neck.

My wolf picks up his pace some again, reaches his hand down to rub at my clit, and in minutes, I'm at the edge again.

He leans into my neck and starts biting and sucking across it. When I come around him, I feel him swell in me before finding his release.

As we come, I feel him sucking hard, at one point in my neck. The feeling makes my orgasm come harder until, eventually, he releases my skin and collapses some on me. He nuzzles into my neck before leaning up and kissing me softly.

I glance down at my hands and see some blood. I realize I must have made Jay bleed.

"Fuck, Jay, I'm so sorry," I say, holding up my hands so that he can see the evidence.

"Don't you dare be sorry. That was the hottest thing that's ever happened to me. Wolves love to mark and be marked by their one Aly Kat, and you're mine." He leans forward to lick the hickey he left on my neck to emphasize his point. And even though I'm going to have a massive bruise on my neck, I'm not mad. I love that he wants the world to know I'm his. I want everyone to know he's mine too.

Nineteen

Aly

I wake up the next morning, wrapped up in Jay's arms. I snuggle back into him, rubbing against him as I do.

"Aly Kat, you're starting something we don't have time to finish," Jay whispers.

"Why don't we have time?" I ask back.

"Some of us have class today, including you and Jeremy," Jay answers.

Oh yeah, Jeremy and I have our Feeding Your Soul class today. I wonder how it'll go now that he isn't acting like he hates me. We are permanent partners in that class, which has made it miserable. I imagine we might actually have some fun now.

Right now I'm focused on being wrapped up in Jay's arms with something hard against my back.

"We have time, come on," I say, turning around in his arms. I lean up to kiss him, and he doesn't stop me. I wrap my leg over the top of him, so I can feel his cock against my core.

Bound

He groans into my mouth before tugging my hair, so he can get to my neck.

"We better make it quick or-" but he doesn't get to finish that sentence.

"Come on baby girl, we have to go if we don't want to be late!" Jeremy says.

He sounds bored, but I can feel his emotions. They're a mixture of jealousy, annoyance, and, most of all, excitement. Is he excited to spend time with me?

I lean up to check the time, and sure enough, he's right. We need to leave. Jay and I slept in.

Jay gives me one more peck before saying, "Go, I'll see you later."

I smile at him, then hop up and get dressed. I need to grab some more clothes and Bailey if I'm going to keep staying here.

* * *

Jeremy and I arrive at class right on time, and I think the teacher is so pleased to see us arrive together that she doesn't even mind.

"Okay class, I have something inspiring for you today! Your work last week for the community garden was exceptional, but today we are going to focus on ourselves."

She pauses to look around the classroom for a response, so I give a bright smile back. It never hurts to have your professor like you.

"Today, you and your partners are going to work on reading each other's emotions! I have these crystals which will help you tune in to your partner's frequency."

She goes around the space, handing out smooth white

crystals to everyone. When she gets back to the front, she keeps explaining what she wants us to do.

"So one partner will write the emotion they're feeling down on a piece of paper and the partner needs to identify it. Then switch. Try thinking of different memories to evoke different feelings!"

I turn to Jeremy, laughing some. With our bond, we feel each other's emotions all day. This exercise will be extremely easy if she comes around to observe.

"Well, maybe this is a good way to work on identifying the feelings from the bond," I whisper.

He nods, but he doesn't seem very excited about it. So I offer to go first. I go through my memories and stop on Bailey. I talk about when I first got him, how it feels to snuggle him, and how much I love him.

Jeremy glares at me before saying, "Love, who are you thinking about?"

I feel jealousy from him. Is he worried I'm already in love with one of the guys? I mean, we are on our way there, but not quite.

"Bailey," I respond, and I feel relief in our bond. "Speaking of Bailey, can we stop to get him and some of my stuff on the way home? Or I can go without you if you need to do something."

He grunts, "I'll go with you. It's a good idea."

Class passes in a blur of this exercise. We both stayed pretty surface level but it was fun to learn some things about Jer. Like he loves and cares about his parents, he really does think of the guys as his best friends, and he's worried about my safety. All things that make me like him a little more.

When we are leaving class, the professor stops us.

"I knew you two would work out your issues. You are meant

to know each other. Continue to develop your bond."

We both nod before hurrying away.

"She's not supernatural, is she?" I ask.

Jeremy shakes his head, "No, she's just kooky."

"How do you know if someone is?" I ask, curious.

"Well, you don't always know. Most of the time, they have something like an aura that gives it away, but if they're powerful enough, they can hide it."

That's interesting.

"Do I have the aura?" I ask.

He pauses, "You don't. It's probably being hidden by someone else."

Who is trying to keep me hidden? I don't get it.

We arrive at my apartment and I let Jeremy and myself in. Anna is sitting on the couch with a boy I haven't met before, and she looks surprised we are here.

She hops up and hugs me, "Hey, Aly! It's so good to see you."

Even if it's only been two days, I get it. I missed her too.

"Hey, I'm going to stay at the guys for a few more days, so I came to get Bailey and some clothes. Is that okay? Maybe we can do coffee or something?"

She nods, then brings her focus to Jeremy, who is glaring daggers at the guy on the couch.

"This is Ryan," she nudges me since she's been talking about Ryan for a while. Ryan, this is my roommate Aly and her... friend Jeremy."

Jeremy clearly doesn't like that title, around what he probably sees as a threat, "boyfriend, actually."

Anna turns to look at me with wide eyes and mouths, "B*oyfriend?*"

"Long story," I whisper in her ear. She nods, knowing I'll tell

Aly

her when we are alone next.

"Nice to meet you," I say to Ryan. He nods from the couch, but his gaze keeps returning to Jeremy, which is fair since he looks like he's going to kill him.

I grab Jeremy's hand, "Well, we are just going to go pack. Have fun out here!"

I pull him into my room, shut the door behind us, and start throwing stuff in a bag.

"I don't like him," Jeremy states, still glaring at the door.

"You don't like anyone," I respond.

I toss my packed bag to him and go to pack up Bailey's stuff. Once I have everything ready, we grab Bailey and head back to the guys' house.

Twenty

Aly

Things finally calm down enough with my bond with Jeremy that I can leave the house and go home. I don't want to stay apart long but for the past month I've been able to do every other night, so I'm not leaving Anna alone too much.

I've still made sure to watch every episode of our show, Big House, with her, so we haven't had any issues. I think she might believe it's a little weird, but she likes the guys and is into my relationship with them.

We are hanging out now, doing homework before I head to the guys' house tonight. I can already start to feel the uncomfortable itch that tells me I need to be closer to Jeremy, so I'll have to leave soon. I get really cranky if I ignore it.

I take Bailey back and forth with me every day, and luckily, he's been doing excellent with that. We still have no idea what he is or what I am. Our research has led nowhere. The guys have all gone home to borrow more books, except Jeremy. His

Aly

parents would know he's bonded, and he's not ready to tell them yet. None of the guys want anyone from the supernatural world to know since things are so uncertain. I think they're being overprotective of me, but who am I to say something? I don't understand their world.

"So, how are things with Ryan?" I ask. She's been quiet about him, which means she actually likes him.

"Good, I would say we should all hang out, but I don't think Jeremy likes him."

I roll my eyes, "Jeremy doesn't like anyone. Maybe we can all do something sometime?"

"Sure, let's plan something," she responds, and she looks excited. She wants this, so I need to put more effort into knowing Ryan.

"I know! We can invite them all over for Big House! It's casual and doesn't require much effort since we will mostly be watching a show."

She beams back, "That sounds great! I'll ask him. Hey, what are your plans for Thanksgiving?" she asks, changing the subject.

"Uh, nothing. I'll just be here," I say. I wonder if the guys will be going home. I'll have to ask them. "Are you going home to your parents?" I ask.

"Yeah, and you know you are always welcome," she says.

One year, I did go back with her, and while her family was so nice and welcoming, it was just sad for me to see such a happy family enjoying the holiday when mine wanted nothing to do with me.

"Thanks, Anna, but not this year. Anyways, I've got to get going," I say, hopping up and packing my bag.

"Are you going to the boys?" she asks, and I nod yes.

"Have fun!"

"Thanks, and let me know what Ryan says about Big House!" I say as I head out the door.

The walk to their place is quick, and when I get there, Nic answers the door.

"Hey princess, how are you?" he asks as he leans in for a sweet kiss.

"I'm good, Nic, how are you?" I ask.

"Better now," he responds, and I blush. He makes me feel so sexy all the time.

"Where is everyone else?" I ask. I know Jeremy is at least here somewhere because I feel better. The itch to be closer to him is almost completely gone. It wants some contact, but it's bearable now.

"Kiran, Jax, and Jay are out but, as I'm sure you know, Jeremy is here somewhere. I think he's studying for a big test. So it's just you and I for now, what shall we do?" he asks with a wink. I lean up to kiss him, and he pulls me upstairs with him.

When we get to his room, he shuts the door and grabs me around the waist, pulling me in close before dropping his lips to mine. He kisses me hungrily, and I moan into his mouth.

He starts unbuttoning the shirt I'm wearing, one button at a time. His knuckles brush against my skin as he goes.

Once the shirt is fully open, he pulls it off over my shoulders and drops it to the ground. He brings his head down to lick and nip at my nipples, and they harden to stiff points. He unbuckles my pants and pushes them down my body while he continues sucking on my nipples. I help by kicking my jeans off, and he bites down hard enough to make me gasp.

He gives me a dirty laugh while he strips his clothes off, leaving us both naked. I moan at seeing his cock freed in front of me and give it a few pumps. Seeing and feeling his stiff cock, makes me clench with need.

Nic sits back on the bed and tugs me so I'm straddling him. He moves me back and forth, rubbing his cock through my slit, coating him in my arousal. He rubs his hands down my spine, and I arch into him more.

"You are so sexy Aly. I'm so damn lucky," he whispers in my ear.

We start kissing like we are trying to merge into one being. His lips are all over mine, nipping and biting before sucking to soothe the sting.

He stands up, lifting me with him before turning around and bringing me back down on the bed with him on top.

He rubs against me and keeps kissing every inch of me. Nic kisses my wrist, up my arm, and to my neck. He pays more attention to behind my ear, which is so damn sensitive I'm writhing under him. Then, he does the same on the other side.

He goes back to my nipples, then kisses down my stomach, but stops before he reaches the best part. He lifts my leg and kisses up one leg and then down the other. Spending more time anywhere that gets a reaction out of me.

"Damn, you're delicious. I could eat every inch of you, princess."

He rubs his hands along my body before circling my opening.

"Do you want me?" he asks, teasing me.

"You know I do, so bad, Nic, please."

"Open yourself up wide for me, princess," he commands, and I comply.

I bring my hands down and open myself up for him so he can see everything. He looks at me like I'm the sexiest thing in the world, and any shyness I feel disappears.

Bound

He rubs his cock up and down, gathering my juices before slowly slipping inside. He goes in a little, then pulls out before pushing in further. Slowly, he works his way inside me inch by inch.

"You're so damn tight, princess," he pushes the rest of the way in, bottoming out in me, "but I know you can take me."

I whimper and try to start moving, but he only lets me for a second before grabbing my hips and stopping me. He is running this show and I'm just along for the ride.

When he's satisfied that I understand I can't move, he starts pumping into me slowly, at first, before picking up his pace. He's hitting me right in my g-spot, and it's not long before I'm ready to come.

I look up at him with a plea in my eyes, and he answers it.

"Come."

I shatter around him, moaning for the world to hear, and I don't care. He keeps going, working me through it until he's wrung so much pleasure from me that I can't breathe.

He lifts my hips off the edge of the bed, holding my weight in his hands and changing the angle. When he starts moving again, at this new angle, I think I've died and gone to heaven. It feels so damn amazing and every nerve in me is being stimulated. It's not long before I'm ready to come again, and Nic already has me conditioned to turn to him for permission.

"Come Aly, come all over my cock and moan my name so loud no one has a doubt who owns you."

And I do. I scream Nic's name as I come. I'm blissed out on pleasure and out of my mind. When he comes down to kiss me, I bite his lip hard. Hard enough to draw blood, but he just chuckles and keeps going.

"Damn, princess, did I make you feral?"

Aly

All I can do is nod. I finally come down from my orgasm with the taste of his blood in my mouth. It's oddly hot and erotic, not something I've experienced before.

Nic pumps into me a few more times before coming himself, shouting my name and gripping me to him like he never wants this to end. And I don't either.

He's holding me close, and I plan to stay like this as long as possible, content in his arms. I feel a sharp tug in my chest like a band snapping. Then, I'm overcome with emotions that don't belong to me: shock, awe, fear, and, most of all, confusion.

Nic leans back suddenly and looks at me with shock written all over his face.

"Do you feel that?" he asks.

And without him having to explain, I know what he means. It's another bond. I can feel Nic like I can feel Jeremy—right next to each other in my soul. And while it feels right to have this with Nic, I'm confused as well. How did this happen?

I feel a tingling run down my right arm, and my eyes shoot to it as Nic's hand clutches his chest.

The same mating mark Jeremy has appears on Nic, crossing arrows over his chest, and a sense of pride fills me that he's marked by me.

I peer down at my arm to see the most beautiful swirls, of what looks like pure magic, run down it. It's full of color, blues, purples, and greens all mixing together to form new colors. It's incredible, and when I touch it tentatively, it feels exactly like Nic and his magic. The mark is moving in random ways like a piece of Nic's magic lives in me.

He stares at it in awe and full of pride. He slowly lifts his hand to touch it, running his finger down it slowly, following some swirls. It instantly turns me on and makes me want him again.

How did this happen?

That confusion is quickly replaced by anger. Did Nic do this? Did he bond with me without my knowledge?

He must feel that change in my attitude because he grabs my face, ensuring I'm staring into his eyes.

"I don't know how this happened, Aly. I'm as shocked as you. Feel my emotions. While I'm happy to have the bond, I'm confused as fuck as to how it happened."

And he's right. I can feel that. So, if he didn't do it, how did it happen?

Twenty-One

Nicoli

I can feel Aly's anger simmering down, and I know she believes me. I sag with relief. I don't want her to think I sprang another mate bond on her without a choice.

I really have no idea how this happened. I didn't use any magic, let alone the mating spell.

I can't say this isn't the best feeling in the world, though. I have my bond with Aly, she's officially my mate and nothing can come between us. In my eyes, she's been my mate since I met her, but now it's official.

It's crazy to experience the bond. You hear about it, but everyone says you need to experience it yourself. I understand why. It would be impossible to describe the soul-deep connection I have to her and her to me. I feel like we've become one.

"Nic, how do mages usually mate?" Aly asks, and I realize this is a conversation we should have had sooner. After we figure this out and come to terms with things, we will all need to sit down and talk about it. We don't want any accidents happening again.

"There's a specific spell. If I had done it, you would have heard me chanting, and I wasn't even using magic," I respond.

She nods like she understands, but I know she doesn't, because I don't either. How could we be mated without me doing that?

Then it hits me and I realize what an idiot I've been. We've all been. We keep theorizing that Aly is supernatural, but we haven't thought about what that means. You only need to complete one side of the mating to be mated. Like how Aly and Jeremy mated the demon way.

Aly and I have probably just mated based on her species. But that still doesn't tell me how, because we didn't do any mating ritual I know.

"Aly, I think we mated based on your species. We've been thinking about it based on us guys and what we are but without knowing what you are, we don't know for sure how you mate. We assumed it would be like one of us, but clearly, it's something else."

"Oh shit, so that really does mean there's something more to me. But if I'm not like one of you, what could I be?" she asks. It's an excellent question, one I don't know the answer to.

"I don't know, but maybe you're some sort of hybrid or something lesser known. We will just have to prioritize this more," I say, and she nods in agreement.

She nuzzles into my chest, and we both feel content at the contact. I need to tell her how I feel about this so nothing like what happened with Jeremy happens to us.

"Aly, I'm so fucking happy to be mated to you. I know we didn't plan on it, that it wasn't a conscious decision, but I don't

Nicoli

regret it. You're my mate, and I love that."

I can feel my heart beating out of my chest. What if she doesn't feel the same or doesn't want the bond? It's incredibly vulnerable to be in this situation with Aly, and I understand Jeremy a little better now.

"Oh, Nic, no, I didn't expect this to happen, but I can't be upset. It feels incredible to have this bond with you. You've always been there for me since the beginning, and you've become one of my best friends. I'm grateful you're my mate. Please relax," she says.

I realize she can feel my nerves through the bond, but her words have eased them. I wrap her up tight in my arms and bring her close to me. I hold my mate tight in my arms and enjoy the moment.

"The guys are going to be so jealous," I say.

She shakes a little with laughter. "They're going to be mad it keeps happening! I need to know what all the ways to mate are so the rest can be conscious decisions."

And I agree, "Let's get them all together, and we can talk through how each species mate. We can talk about what happened here, too, and see if anyone has any ideas. It can't be sex in general because this isn't our first time, so something else must have happened."

"I agree. Let's just enjoy some time together now, though. We did just mate, and I just want to be as close to you as possible," she responds, and it melts my heart.

"That sounds great, Aly," I respond, hugging her tighter to me.

"Nic, can we keep the wall down? I want to feel the bond fully with you. We can put it up if we ever need to," she asks. I know she and Jeremy had trouble with that, and I want to do whatever she wants here.

"Of course, I would love that. I don't want to dull what I'm feeling at all. I want to enjoy every second of this bond with you, Aly."

I can feel her smile into my chest and her happiness through the bond. I'm so damn grateful to whatever force brought Aly to me. She's my whole world, and I'll do whatever it takes to keep it that way.

There's a lot we need to do, including find out what she is, but at this moment, it's all worth it. It'll always be worth it to have my perfect mate with me.

Twenty-Two

Aly

Nic and I finally head downstairs after some quality time together. It felt valuable to get what Jeremy and I didn't the first time. Time to cement the bond and just enjoy it. I'm nervous to tell the rest of the guys. Jeremy probably won't care since he already has his bond but the other three will probably be jealous. And I completely get that, but I want the rest of the bonds to come naturally, not be forced.

As soon as we walk in the kitchen, hand in hand, four heads jerk up immediately. Jeremy's smirk is knowing, he probably felt it when it happened but the other three are shocked. I'm not sure how they could tell right away but then I remember my arm. I glance down at the new, beautiful mark and realize any supernatural I meet now will know I'm mated to a mage.

Jeremy's isn't as visible, but he did say I will give off a dark vibe to other supernaturals to let them know I'm mated to a demon, which is more subtle than Nic's mark.

Bound

"What happened?" Jeremy asks since the other three are shocked silent.

"We don't actually know," Nic responds.

That breaks them out of it and Jay and Kiran shout over each other.

"What do you mean you don't know?" Jay shouts.

"How can you not know?" Kiran asks.

Jeremy's eyes go a little dark and I can see his demon seeping through.

"Did you do it without her permission, Nic?" he growls, and while I appreciate his protectiveness of me, I don't want this to get out of hand.

I step forward and their eyes all shoot to me before going back to glaring at Nic.

"Calm down, he didn't do it," I start but Jay cuts me off.

"Did you tell her that?" Then he turns his attention to me. "Aly Kat, a mating bond is a conscious choice for a mage. He has to recite a spell for it to click."

I raise my hand to stop him, "I know, okay? He explained that, and he didn't say any spell."

"Well, how could you have a mate bond then?" Kiran asks.

Jax has been silent up until this point, but a look of total clarity comes over his face before he says, "Aly."

Kiran shoots his brother a glare, "Yes, Aly is right there. Are you okay? We've been talking about her this whole time."

Jax rolls his eyes, "No, it's Aly. We keep ignoring the fact that Aly is supernatural too. She must have triggered the bond if Nic didn't, and come on guys, you know and trust Nic, think about what you're accusing him of."

Kiran, Jay, and Jeremy give Nic an apologetic face, and he forgives them with a nod. I think he understands how crazy this all is for all of us.

"So, is that what you two think happened?" Jay asks.

I turn to Nic since he thought of the theory first, and he steps in. "Yes, we do, but we don't know how. It wasn't triggered like any species I know."

They all stare at me curiously, and suddenly, I feel awkward. What does that mean for me?

"It's okay, baby, we will figure it out, I promise," Kiran says.

I give him a weak smile in response.

"I think we need to talk about how each species mates, so there are no more surprises," Nic suggests.

"And then you can tell us what happened when your mating bond was triggered in case it helps us figure it out or avoid something in the future until we are ready," Jax says, giving me a soft smile. I love that he wants to respect my choice in all this.

I nod, "So I know demons mate by sharing blood, mages recite a spell, what about the rest of you?"

Jay starts, "Well, for shifters, it takes a bite. A claiming bite on the neck, where I break the skin, and it becomes permanent. It serves as the mating mark, like your arm for Nic or the pentagram for Jeremy."

My nerves must show on my face at that because Jay gets up and walks over to me. He cups my face in his hands and leans in to kiss me.

"I promise it's pleasurable, Aly Kat. As my mate, you'll probably be craving bites from me all the time."

My pussy clenches at the sound of that, and I find the idea does turn me on. I lean in to kiss him again, and it gets heated quickly. He tugs me closer to him, fusing our bodies and giving my bottom lip a small bite. I moan into his mouth, and I'm about to start grinding on him when a throat clears.

"As hot as this is, we should really finish this conversation," Nic says.

We break apart, but Jay wraps himself around me from behind while I face the room again. He's nuzzling my neck and giving me small bites which are distracting but I love it so much I don't complain.

I consider Kiran and Jax to see what they'll say about fae. I wonder if it's different for light and dark?

Kiran seems a little unsure like he's afraid I won't like what he has to say, so I encourage him to go first and get it out of the way.

"I have to speak a chant in fae then," he pauses before putting his shoulders back and continuing, "before I have to send some of my darkness into you to bind us together."

I pull away from Jay and go to Kiran, wrapping my arms around him when I get there.

"I'm not afraid of your darkness, Kiran, and when it's time, I'll be happy to bond with you."

He relaxes at that, and I wonder how long he's been worried about my reaction. I turn to look at Jax, who is smiling, glancing between Kiran and me. I bet he knew Kiran was concerned about it.

"Same for me but different words, and it's some of my light," he says.

I lean over and kiss Jax on the cheek before saying, "Well, I can't wait for that either. None of those seem like they could happen accidentally easily, so that's good."

Nic looks at me pointedly. "But we still don't know how you triggered the bond with me."

"What were you doing?" Jay asks.

Aly

He has sneakily made his way back over and wrapped himself around me again.

I can feel the blush spreading across my face, and Jeremy chuckles from across the room.

It hits me. "Oh my God, you know? You can feel it?"

He straight up laughs aloud now. "Yeah, baby girl, I can feel your emotions. Of course, I know. Don't worry, I don't mind." He finishes with a wink, and I relax a little.

The other three catch on and start chuckling, too. Then, Kiran turns to me with a horrified expression.

"Is that what triggered it? Does having sex create the bond for you?" he asks.

He's probably terrified of having to wait until we are ready for the bond to have sex, but lucky for him, it's not that.

"No, it can't be," I say.

"Why not?" Kiran asks.

And I'm feeling shy again. I hope no one is mad about this. I guess it's an excellent way to see how this sharing is going. I look to Nic, who just smiles all smugly back at me.

"Oh," Kiran says, "it wasn't your first time."

Then he starts laughing and offers a high-five to Nic, who ignores it. Jay squeezes me, and Jax gives me a soft smile, and I relax. They are okay with things.

"Yeah," I say "so it couldn't be that, but it did happen right at the end."

Jax looks awkward but speaks up anyway, "Could it have to do with the ending?"

It takes me a minute to realize he means Nic coming, and I think back to the first time we had sex, but he came in me then, too. I shake my head no, and he goes back to thinking.

"Did you say anything?" Jeremy asks.

"Nothing out of the ordinary, definitely not something in another language," I respond.

"Maybe we should focus on trying to figure out what Aly is. There may be more accounts out there of people who didn't fall in one of the categories we know," Jax suggests, and we all agree quickly. That's probably the best solution. I'm not sure we will get anywhere trying to figure out what happened between Nic and me.

Now that that's decided, we all break apart to go our separate ways, but Kiran stops me before I make it out of the room.

He grabs my hand and gives it a little tug, encouraging me to turn around. I do, and I end up settled in his arms.

"What's up, Kiran?" I ask, curious why he wanted to talk to me alone.

He seems nervous, the second time today for my confident guy. I guess he gets nervous about how I will react to things.

"Well, I was wondering if I could take you on a date. Just because we are mates doesn't mean I shouldn't wine and dine you."

I swoon and melt right then and there. I jump up into his arms, and he catches me easily with both hands cupping my ass.

"Oh, Kiran! That sounds great, thank you!"

I lean in and give him a kiss, which he reciprocates enthusiastically. He looks so happy at my response.

"Great baby, I know you have your date with Jeremy first, but let's plan to go out after that. Maybe the next weekend?" he asks.

"That sounds great!" I respond and go back in for another kiss.

I mean for it to be a peck, full of excitement but as soon as

Aly

my lips touch his I'm a goner. He brings a hand up to the back of my head, holding me tight to him as he expertly works my lips with his.

I'm still in his arms, and I can feel him growing harder against me the longer we kiss. He tangles his tongue with mine, licking every inch of me like I'm the best taste in the world.

I understand the urge because he is delicious to me. Like my own personal drug, they all are. He sucks my tongue into his mouth before slowly trailing his teeth over it as he pulls away.

He puts his forehead on mine and stares me in the eyes. "I could get lost in you forever, and I wouldn't ever want someone to find me."

I melt into another puddle.

"I feel the same, Kiran. It's so easy to get completely lost in you, too. You and your lips," I say with a wink, and he responds with a real peck this time.

He sets me down carefully, making sure I'm steady on my feet before backing up.

"Come on, they're probably wondering where we are."

He leads the way out of the room, holding my hand, as we go off to try to figure out what I am.

With the guys by my side, that seems a little less scary.

Twenty-Three

Aly

We are all gathered around the guys' books about supernaturals. They all go to their rooms and gather anything they have for us to look through. Naturally, Jax has the most, so Kiran starts helping him after his own contribution.

"Why so many books?" I ask once everyone is back in the room.

"Well, we've all amassed books about our kind to help us learn and train with our powers. We learned how to control them when we were younger and these helped us. There's no internet for supernaturals, so any knowledge is passed down through books," Jax answers.

I nod in thanks for his answer. That makes sense.

"So where do we start?" I ask.

The guys all look around at each other, unsure of the answer. Eventually, Jax steps up with an idea. "Well, now that the spell isn't on you, have you noticed anything strange happening?

Aly

Anything you may have done or felt?"

I think it through for a minute, but everything has felt normal besides the mate bonds.

"Honestly, no, but I'm not sure I would know when it's already been so much between the two mate bonds."

Jax nods and Nic and Jeremy appear a little guilty, which is silly. I reach across the table and grab both their hands with mine.

"I'm not complaining, and I don't regret that we have them. I'm just saying crazy things have been happening or I've been feeling things I'm not used to because of it."

I squeeze their hands before pulling away and leaning back in my seat. They both seem happier, and it's a good reminder that they could use reassurance sometimes, too.

"Well, another clue is the mating mark Aly gave us," Nic points out.

Everyone stares at him pointedly, and he lifts his shirt to show the marking on his heart. To me, the mark feels strong and fierce while also loving. I feel strongly connected to it, so it must mean something important to my species.

"Has anyone ever seen anything like it?" Kiran asks.

There's silence around the table.

"It's nothing like all of our marks. The closest it would be is to Jeremy's, but if Aly was a demon, that would represent her pentagon, and it's not that," Jay finally says.

"Let's see if we can find anything in these books like it," Jax suggests, opening the first book in front of him.

"Before we start, there's one more thing I want to address," Nic says, and all eyes turn to him.

"What is it?" I ask.

"Well, I don't want to concern you, Aly, but being supernatural can be dangerous, so I think we should start training you in self-defense while we do research."

A knot forms in my stomach. I don't mind the idea of learning to defend myself, but I don't like the idea of the guys being in danger.

"Why is it dangerous?" I ask.

They all freeze before Nic answers, "I don't want you to worry, because we will always protect you but there's another supernatural race called hunters and like their name suggests, they hunt the rest of us. They are dangerous and you should always be prepared."

There is a whole species dedicated to hunting other supernaturals? Why would that be?

"It's actually why we left our old university. They found out there was a large supernatural presence and they came for us," Jay says carefully.

"Are there more supernaturals here?" I ask, worried the same thing might happen again.

"No, there's not. That's actually why we picked it, so it should be safer," Kiran says.

Before I can ask another question, Jeremy chimes in, "We are going to protect you, Aly. You don't need to worry."

He sounds so sure, and I can feel his confidence through the bond, so I let it reassure me.

"Okay," I whisper.

"Great, so we will set up a schedule for training. Anything else before we start looking through these books?" Nic asks.

I have one more thing, something I'm afraid to voice aloud, but I need to know.

"Actually, yes. Is there a chance I'm a hunter?"

They all freeze and gaze at me in horror before quickly

Aly

shutting that idea down.

"No way, Aly Kat, we would be mortal enemies, not mates!" Jay says.

"It's not possible. There has never been a mating between hunters and anyone else. I don't even think they mate," Jax reasons.

"You wouldn't be able to sit here calmly in the same room as us if you were, baby, don't worry," Kiran adds.

Jeremy just nods his head in agreement like there's nothing more to possibly say.

"There's no chance, so don't let that worry I can feel spread. It's not possible, but we will find out what you are. So let's start doing just that," Nic commands.

We all grab a book and start looking. The guys move much faster than me, as I'm sure they already know all this. But for me, it's all new and I can't help getting sidetracked by all the information. I'll have to read all of these over time to help me catch up and understand the guys and what they are better.

We work for hours without finding anything and eventually call it a night, promising to keep looking.

It's disappointing we didn't make any progress, but I know the guys won't give up, and neither will I. We must learn what I am for both my sake and theirs. If I don't know what my powers are, I could be putting them in danger, and that's unacceptable to me.

* * *

"Okay, it's time to go over some basics. You don't have any training in self-defense, right?" Nic asks.

We are all gather in their basement gym for my lesson in

self-defense. The guys are adamant that I learn how to defend myself in case they're ever not around.

"Right," I respond.

"Okay, so let's start with weak points. If you need to defend yourself, you start by aiming for their eyes, nose, throat, groin, or knees. Okay?" he asks.

"Yes, got it."

"Okay, so start by hitting me in one of those areas," he directs.

I'm not sure where to start, but the knees feel like an ideal place. Instead of the awkward move I'm planning, I perfectly execute a leg sweep that gets Nic down on the mat.

"Whoa!" Kiran shouts.

"Uh, I thought you said you've never trained in self-defense? That was an advanced move, Aly," Jay points out.

I look up at them from where I'm staring at Nic on the mat with horror on my face.

"I haven't, it just happened. It was like my body knew how to do it, even though my mind didn't."

I put my hand out to help Nic up. "I'm sorry," I whisper.

He gets up and pulls me into a hug. "There's nothing to be sorry about. It seems you naturally have a gift here, or someone has trained you and spelled you to forget."

"Again," Jeremy adds dryly.

We run through some more exercises and I'm incredible, I hold my own against two of the guys at once. Without them using their power, of course. When they ask me to describe the move or how to execute it, I can't. I can only do it, not consciously think about it.

"Do you guys think my parents have something to do with this?" I ask.

They all share a look before all eyes turn to Nic.

Aly

"Yes, we do. I'm sorry, Aly," he responds.

Even though I'm not close with them, they're still my parents. It feels like a betrayal if they're behind all of this.

"Should I ask them?" I ask hesitantly.

"No!" They all shout.

"Sorry, Aly, but if they're behind this, they didn't want you to know. Who knows what they'll do if you confront them," Jax adds.

"Aly, a while back, you told us you don't know what your parents do. Is that true?" Kiran asks.

For the first time, I realize how strange it is that I don't know what they do for a living. I realize how often I should have pushed or asked them again but decided not to.

I glance up at them, "I think part of the memory spell was in play because I never pushed and I accepted their non-answers. So that means it's something supernatural, right?"

"Probably," Nic answers. They're all watching me closely, clearly realizing how crazy this is. My parents are or do something related to supernaturals, and I have no idea what. They want to keep me away from it with all these spells, but why?

We finish training and it's clear there is nothing for them to teach me. We agree to keep practicing together, though, and see if anything else comes up.

I'm about to head back to the apartment to watch Big House with Anna. I asked the guys to stay behind because Anna texted me that Ryan couldn't come. We will have to try for another time. I'm bummed, but Jeremy seemed excited at the news. He stands by the fact that he doesn't like Ryan, but from the few times I've met him, I think he's great. That's probably why Jeremy doesn't like him.

They all give me a quick kiss goodbye and sad eyes for leaving.

"Don't look at me like that! I'll be back tomorrow," I promise.

The more time we spend together, the harder it is to leave. I want them with me all the time, but I refuse to get completely wrapped up in my relationships. Even if it's an unconventional relationship with five guys, I need to maintain a life outside it.

Anna has been super cool with me being gone so much, but I still need to prioritize time with her. Plus, I need that time with Anna. It helps me work through my feelings with the guys.

Twenty-Four

Aly

My time with just Anna and me was great. I ended up staying home a few days with her and just seeing the guys during the day. Oddly enough, both bonds have settled more since I bonded with Nic. I thought I would be starting all over again, but I'm not.

I'm heading over to the guys' place to spend some time with Kiran. He asked me for help with math, and I'm looking forward to spending time with him alone.

I get to the door, and before I can knock, Kiran is there, radiating excited energy.

"Aly, you're here! Finally!" He reaches in and gives me a hug and a quick kiss on my cheek before grabbing my hand and dragging me in behind him.

"Hi Kiran, good to see you too," I say with a laugh.

He's practically hauling me behind him, trying to get me to move faster.

"Come on, baby, I need to get you in my room before anyone else realizes you're here and tries to steal you away or join."

"You didn't tell anyone I was coming?" I ask.

He stares at me like I'm crazy, "Of course not! I want some quality time with my girl."

Something in me melts at that. I love him calling me his girl.

"To study," I say sternly.

"Sure, of course, I wouldn't dream of anything else," he responds airily.

We finally make it up to his room, and he shuts the door behind me as soon as I'm through it.

I laugh before glancing around for a spot to settle. He makes the decision easy by sitting on his bed.

I set my backpack down at the end of the bed and take a minute to look around his room. It radiates Kiran, and I love it. It smells like his sweet, oaky scent, emanates comfort, and is full of fun fixtures. He's got random little, colorful statues mixed around and posters on the walls.

"What do you think?" He interrupts my perusal by asking.

"I love it, it's so you, Kiran," I respond, coming back to the bed.

I sit next to him, but that's not enough for him. He picks me up and settles me on his lap.

"I'm not sure this is an optimal studying position," I point out.

"It'll motivate me to work. You know what else would motivate me to study harder?" he asks, sounding mischievous, and I can't help playing along.

"What?"

"Well, if I get something right, one of us has to take off a piece of clothing. What better motivator could there be?" He winks.

Aly

I laugh, not sure if he's serious or not but when I turn back to see him, he's staring at me with his eyebrows raised and hopeful.

I think it through for a minute. It'll probably be distracting for studying, but it sounds fun, so I decide to try it.

"Okay, we can do that but if you get too distracted, then all the clothes come back on!" I say and he agrees with a nod.

I reach over to my bag, pull out our textbook for the math class, and open it to the right page.

"Okay, first question," I point to the first sample question in our textbook, and he gets out a notebook to work on it.

He takes a few minutes, and I watch him as he goes. He's so close, but he makes a minor mistake at the end that changes the answer. He glances at me and I give him a slight cringe and shake my head no.

"Sorry you were so close, though! It was right here, you forgot-" but he cuts me off.

"I forgot to carry the decimal, damn it!" But he doesn't sound too mad about it, and I like his optimism.

"That's great you knew what was wrong! Here, try the next one."

He starts on the next one, and this time, he gets it right. When I smile and tell him it's correct, he stares at me expectantly.

"You said one of us had to take something off. You go first," I say.

He complies right away, tugging his shirt off and tossing it to the floor. I try to ogle him, catching some muscles and tattoos, but before I can look too hard, he tisks at me.

"Focus up baby, don't get distracted!" he calls me out.

My eyes shoot up to his, and I give him a guilty smile. "You're right, do problem three."

He gets that one right, too, and I'm impressed. I thought he was going to struggle a little more than this, but maybe he's been working on it.

He looks at me, and this time, I comply by reaching down and taking off a sock. He rolls his eyes but starts the next problem. He gets the next couple right, and he loses both his socks, and I lose my other one.

When he gets the next one right, the clear option is my shirt, so I slowly take it off, teasing him as I go. I reveal a sexy black bra with lace, and he lets out a groan when he sees it.

"Damn, baby."

I lean back against him, feeling his hot skin against mine, and it feels like heaven. The skin-to-skin contact makes our connection stronger. He's still staring at me so I imitate what he said to me earlier.

"Focus up, baby, don't get distracted!"

He bursts out laughing, then he leans in close and whispers in my ear, "You're way more distracting than I am, but good try."

He pulls back and winks before doing the next problem.

Kiran pulls off his pants next, leaving him in his black boxers, and I can feel his bulge when I settle back on his lap. It feels very impressive, like intimidatingly impressive.

I give a little wiggle on his lap while he works on the next problem and he groans into my ear.

"You better stop that, or studying will be over," he whispers.

I freeze right away and settle back into him. He gets this one right and I'm shocked he has only gotten the first one wrong. Then it hits me.

"You studied before I got here!" I accuse.

He gives me a very fake innocent look and brings his hand

Aly

up to his chest in mock horror.

"Me? Plan this ahead of time? Never! Now take off those pants, baby," he emphasizes that by dropping a kiss on my lips.

I think about fighting it since he cheated, but I'm having fun, and I want to see where this goes.

I shimmy my leggings off, leaving me in matching lace and black panties.

"Oh, damn."

He leans in and gives me a scorching kiss, wrapping his arms around me and pulling me in close. He rubs his hands up and down my skin.

"Your skin is so soft," he whispers before kissing the response off my lips.

Kiran reaches down to cup my ass and flip me so I'm straddling him. I can feel his cock through his boxers, and it is rock-hard now. I grind against it some, and we both moan.

"Do you want me to take care of you, baby?" he asks, nipping up and down my neck.

"Yes, please," I respond.

He leans forward, pushing me down on the bed with him on top of me. His fingers trail down my body until he's rubbing me over the top of my panties.

"Fuck baby, I can feel how wet you are. You soaked your panties," he says before diving in for more kisses.

He starts rubbing circles around my clit until I'm squirming under him.

"Do you want more, baby?" he asks.

"Yes," I say, reaching down to take my panties off.

Kiran smacks my hand away, and instead of pulling my panties down, he just rips them right off.

I gasp in shock, but instead of yelling at him, I just enjoy how sexy that was. It was really fucking hot, and what is one more pair of panties.

He circles two of his fingers around my opening before slowly working his way inside of me.

He pumps in and out slowly and measured until I'm dying for him to move faster. He picks up on my impatience and starts moving faster until I'm so close.

He abruptly stops, pulling his fingers out, and I scream in protest.

"Kiran! Don't stop!"

"Shh, don't worry, I've got you," he responds.

He leans down, bringing his mouth to my core before he blows on me. I can feel myself clenching while he does it, feeling so empty and needing more contact.

"Kiran!" I groan.

He sits up and smiles at me before he leans back down and digs right in. He starts licking and sucking me with vigor until I'm right back on the brink.

He stabs his tongue inside of me, and right when I'm about to come, he eases off again.

I'm about to actually scream, and I'm sure that will draw the attention of whoever else is home. That will teach him to tease me so badly. But he stabs his fingers back in me and sucks on my clit hard until I go off.

I moan his name and enjoy the pleasure pulsing through me as he works me through my orgasm.

When I finally come back to earth, I look up and see him leaning over me with the biggest smile.

I smile back, then lean up to kiss him, tasting myself on his lips. I push his left shoulder, encouraging him to flip. I'm sure I couldn't move him if he didn't let me, but he does with an amused smile.

I kiss him, then start kissing down his body. Paying special attention to his neck and abs before kissing his v down to the edge of his boxers.

I pull his boxers down and toss them aside. His cock springs free, and it's so damn big I'm worried about taking him in my mouth.

He sees my worry and does the sexiest chuckle, saying, "Don't worry, baby, you can take me."

I give him a confident stare, then innocently say, "I know."

But he doesn't let me win. "Oh, are you just realizing that since Jax and I are identical, you have two of these to deal with?"

That does shock me. He's right, and it's hot as hell that I've gotten this insight into Jax before even being with him. Damn, that boy does not need to be shy.

"Oh, that turns you on, baby?" he asks.

I respond by leaning in and taking him right into my mouth. I take him as deep as I can, and when he bumps into the back of my throat, I swallow instead of panicking. I bring my right hand up to pump what I can't take, and he moans. That shut him up.

I pump him, licking the tip, then swallowing him back down again. He brings his hand to the back of my head, gripping my hair. He starts controlling my pace and I love it. I love knowing I'm giving him exactly what he wants.

He swells some in my mouth, so I know he's getting closer, and I suck even harder.

"Fuck!" he shouts, and then he's coming down my throat. I struggle to swallow everything, but I manage to lick him clean.

"Damn baby, that was hot as fuck. I never want to know how

you learned to do that so well," he says, tensing at the end.

I lean up to kiss him. I don't want his thoughts of the past to ruin this moment, so I whisper something I know he'll love.

"I was made for you, Kiran. Of course, I know how to take care of you."

His eyes flare with heat, and he leans in and kisses me so passionately that my toes curl. He pulls me in close to him, and I settle into his arms.

"Damn right you were, baby," he whispers, kissing the top of my head.

Twenty-Five

Aly

It feels crazy to be in classes like my world hasn't completely changed. I don't know how the guys act like normal humans all the time, but I guess it's just crazier for me because it's new.

People keep staring curiously at Nic's mating mark on my arm. Nic spelled it so it would look like a regular tattoo to humans, but I wanted to keep it visible in some way.

It was a strong instinct in me, I am protective of it and want to show it off, even if humans won't understand what it means. I could feel how pleased Nic was when I told him that, which made it even better. We had some hot sex where he was very possessive to show how happy it made him. I make a mental note to remind him of it again, next time we are alone, so we can have a round two.

My dirty thoughts are interrupted by the professor emphasizing something while he lectures, and I try to tune back in, but my thoughts quickly slip to Jeremy's mark. I wish I could show his off as well, but I understand that his pentagram can't just be shown to everyone. I love what a show of trust it is in your mate to have it be a demon's mark. They carry an essential piece of you and I'm honored to have that for Jeremy. Maybe if I tell him that next time we are alone, things will heat up between us?

I crave that, so I make a mental note to do that and try to think of other ways to seduce Jeremy.

The next thing I know, everyone is standing up to leave the room since class ended, and I didn't notice. I rush to pack up my bag, and Jax laughs at my startled look.

"Daydreaming?" he asks.

I blush, and it must be clear what I'm thinking about because he blushes too, but instead of avoiding the topic, he embraces it. I love it.

"What are you thinking about, Aly? Nothing inappropriate, I'm sure!" he says in mock horror, a little too loud, just to embarrass me.

People glance over as they pass us to leave and I feel my face grow hotter.

"I cannot believe you just did that, Ajax Stone! I will get you back for that!"

He throws his hands up quickly, "No, no retaliation needed. I'll be good, I promise!"

I finally have my bag packed, so I stand up and lean in close to him. I give him a sweet kiss on the cheek before saying, "Not too good, I hope."

He turns bright red and looks around the room and my revenge is complete. But I also kind of mean it. I want to move at his pace, but I'm excited to see what things are like with Ajax at the next level.

Aly

I grab his hand and we head out the door on our way to the next class we share with everyone. I'm so glad I get this extra time with the guys in our classes. Between the actual classes and studying together, it's a decent amount.

As we make our way across campus, I see lots of people wave or give bro nods to Jax, which is shocking since the guys seem to stick together and Ajax is so shy. Now that I think about it, they all seem to get lots of hellos and friendly waves, but I never see them talking to anyone else.

"How do you know all these people?" I ask him after the tenth one.

"Oh, I don't, not really. I may have a class with them or something but they are all drawn in by what we are. All of us," he answers.

When I give him a confused look, his face turns less sure. "Does that not happen to you?"

"No, I've always had a harder time making friends or getting people to like me," I answer.

He thinks about it for a minute before giving my hand a reassuring squeeze. "Just another piece to the puzzle. We will figure it out!"

I nod but I don't feel so sure. Why can't I just be a normal supernatural who lines up with one of the guys? They have no idea what I could be and more facts keep pointing to me being strange.

Not that the guys say that. They're always staying positive no matter how much time we spend finding nothing.

Jax must notice my mood drop because he squeezes my hand before changing the subject.

"So, you have your date with Jeremy coming up, are you excited?" he asks.

Bound

I love that I can discuss this with him without it being weird. Who knew having five boyfriends wouldn't be completely strange?

"Yeah, I'm excited, but I have no idea what we are doing," I say before fishing by asking, "Do you?"

"Oh no, even if I did, I wouldn't tell you. If Jeremy wants it to be a surprise, then you'll just have to live with that," he responds.

"If you knew, I bet you'd tell me," I respond.

He blushes. "I probably would, which is probably why Jeremy didn't tell me or any of us."

"Hmm, fair enough," I say.

"It seems like things between you two have been better," he points out.

They have. Since we both decided to try, we have fallen into a natural relationship. I'm hoping this date validates all of that.

"Yeah, we have, it's a lot better than when he hated me," I say.

Jax snorts a laugh. "He never hated you, and you know it."

And he's right, now I do know that. Before we were mates, I would have never believed that boy didn't completely hate me, but now I know what was wrong, and we are moving past things. He's still a grumpy demon, but at least now he's mine.

***

Jeremy and I have our date tonight, and I'm incredibly nervous. I feel like I'm going on my first date ever, which is crazy.

I can feel his nerves through the bond, though, so I know it's not just me.

There's a knock at our front door, and when I answer it, my demon is on the other side. Jeremy is seriously delicious in black jeans and a black button-up. Of course, my demon is in all black, but it's sexy on him. He's looking me over, too, in my skirt and sweater. I think we make a pretty cute couple.

"You ready?" he asks.

"Yup," I say as I grab my purse to head out.

Jeremy surprises me by grabbing my hand and leading me down to his car. He even opens the door for me, and after we both get in, I can't help but comment.

"You're being quite the gentleman."

"Don't expect it to last," he mumbles.

We end up at a fancy restaurant and I feel like Jeremy put a lot of effort into this. That knocks over any walls I have left, and I'm ready to fully embrace him as my mate.

Once we are seated and order some drinks, we just stare at each other. He would probably be comfortable in the silence, but I want to use this opportunity to get to know him better.

"So, what do you like to do for fun?" I ask.

He stares at me like I'm crazy. "Fun?"

"Yeah, you know an emotion that makes you happy? Like video games or bowling?"

He grunts. "I've never been bowling."

"What? Even I've been bowling, we have to go! All of us," I declare.

He rolls his eyes and looks annoyed, but I can feel his amusement through the bond. It's much harder to maintain the aloof bad boy persona when I can feel his emotions.

We keep up the small talk while ordering our meal, and I feel close to him right now. This one-on-one time is what we needed.

I know how I want this date to end, so I make sure he knows it, too. I run my foot up the inside of his leg, but at first, he doesn't comment.

As I keep doing it, I can feel lust building in him.

I run my foot up his leg again, and he stares at me with heat in his eyes.

"You're playing a dangerous game, baby girl."

I wink. "I know."

The sexual tension has just been building up between us for so long. It needs an outlet. I want him bad and I know he wants me too. I can feel his lust for me through the bond, and it's adding to mine. We are compounding on each other until it's almost unbearable.

We finish our meal and I know we are both dying to get out of here and back home. Apparently, the waitress is taking too long because Jeremy stands up before reaching for me.

"Come on, get up," he demands.

I look at him, confused, but decide to go with it. I stand up, and he drags me behind him toward the restrooms.

Jeremy drags me into the bathroom, locking the door behind him.

"Fuck," he groans.

He picks me up and crushes me between him and the wall. My skirt easily lifts, and he presses himself against my panties.

"I can't even think straight around you," he groans.

He moves my panties aside to feel how wet I am.

"You're soaked, baby girl, damn."

He brings those fingers up to his mouth and sucks my taste off of him.

"Delicious, I'll be wanting more of that."

"Later," I groan. I need him in me now.

He reaches to unbutton his pants, pulling them down just enough to release his cock. He lines up with me and thrusts all

Aly

the way in. He's lucky I'm soaked because I can feel how big he is. I feel something scraping against me in the best way, and I gaze up at him in shock.

"You're pierced!"

He releases a dirty laugh before nodding and pounding into me again. Fuck, that piercing feels incredible. It hits me in the G-spot every fucking time.

He brings his face to my shoulder and groans before pulling back and pounding into me again and again. He is hammering me against the door, which is making a lot of noise. He must finally notice it because he pulls me away and turns to the closest wall.

He starts pounding into me again, but this time, it's quieter. He brings his hand down to rub my clit, and I go off around him. He must be on edge because he starts coming as soon as I do. I can feel the hot splash of his come in me, and I moan.

We stay like that for a minute, wrapped up in each other, breathing in the other person. It's heaven finally being connected with him like this.

I move my head out of the crook of his neck and lean it against the wall.

"Damn, can we do that again?" I ask with a wink.

He smirks back at me. "When we get home. I'm pretty sure this whole restaurant heard us, so we should probably go."

I know he's right. We weren't exactly quiet, and it's a nice restaurant. They probably called the cops on us.

"Okay, let's go," I say.

He drops another kiss on my lips before lowering me back to the ground. I grab his hand and we run out of the restaurant after throwing money down at our table.

Twenty-Six

Aly

This past week has been incredible. After our date, I feel so close to Jeremy. We're spending so much time together. But he must part with me tonight because Kiran and I have our date.

Kiran has called me into the living room with everyone else. I'm not sure why, but I trust him.

"What's up?" I ask, looking around at all of them. We've been busy lately, and seeing them all together feels great. We haven't had any fun like the game night we had before I knew we were all mates.

"I have an idea, we've been spending all our spare time together researching, which is very important, but so is growing our bond. So, I was thinking we could do a group date tonight. I will, of course, still want my solo date with you, but I think this is more important."

I feel a huge smile take over my face. This is perfect, and I love that Kiran knew I needed it.

Aly

"I love that idea! Thank you," I say and go sit on his lap to show him how appreciative I am with some kisses.

"What should we do?" Nic asks.

I know just the thing. I look over at Jeremy, and based on his face, I think he knows what I'm about to suggest.

"Well, Jeremy has never been bowling, so I think we should do that!"

The guys all laugh and shoot amused expressions at Jeremy.

"You down for that, Jer? We can never get you to come with us," Jay asks.

Jeremy rolls his eyes. "If that's what Aly wants to do, I'll go."

I give him my biggest smile and send a burst of happiness down the bond. He gives me a soft smile back and I feel like I've won the lottery.

We get to the bowling alley, and Jeremy looks like someone just kicked his puppy. He's brooding about being here but I can feel a twinge of excitement from him.

We all walk up to the counter to get our shoes and balls, then settle in at our lanes. We got two, and we are competing, three versus three. The guys seem excited about being out together, and I love the idea of time as a group. I'm so grateful to Kiran for arranging it.

"Okay, so what are teams?" I ask.

Immediately Kiran and Jay both shout, "I call Aly!"

I roll my eyes at them, "You can't always call dibs on me."

"How else will we decide?" Kiran asks.

Nic steps in, "Well, we should probably try to make the teams even. Jax is the best, and Jeremy has never bowled, so they should be on the same team with someone in the middle."

I look over at Jax and raise my eyebrows. He blushes. I walk over to him and whisper, "You're the best, huh?"

Bound

He lets out a soft laugh, "Yup, best bowler around, what a cool thing to be good at."

"I think it is," I say back with a smile. I turn to the group and speak up, "I'll be with Jax and Jeremy. I'm average."

Nic nods, but Kiran and Jay both pout at me. It's a smart choice, though. Jeremy is only bowling for me, and Jax isn't going to call dibs on time with me. Plus, we are all still together. It's not like anyone else will get less time together.

Nic and Jax put our names in, and I sit next to Jay.

"Consorting with the enemy?" he asks.

Kiran sits on my other side, and with a wink, he says, "I can't believe you didn't choose our team. We are going to destroy you."

"I'll take my chances," I say back to both of them.

Jay wraps an arm around my seat, and we watch as Nic and Jax go. Jax gets a strike, and Nic gets a spare.

Next up are Kiran and Jeremy. Kiran leans in close and gives me a sweet kiss.

"Kiss for luck!" he says as he walks away.

I shout back, "I did not give you any luck! You're on the other team!"

He gets a strike and smirks at me with an I told you so look on his face.

Jeremy knocks seven down, and for his first time, I'm just proud he didn't throw a gutter ball.

Next up, Jay and I. Luckily for our team, I get a strike and Jay a spare. Everyone is surprisingly decent.

The game keeps going the same. Jax gets a strike every time, keeping us neck and neck with Kiran, Jay, and Nic. It comes down to me and Jay at the end. Of course, Kiran doesn't play fair, so while I'm lining up, he comes up behind me. He presses himself against me and leans down to whisper in my ear.

"You look so hot right now. Will you come back to my room when we get home?"

I shiver. I want that so badly that I start imagining everything he could do to me. I want his hands all over me like they are now but without clothes. He's running his hands up and down my sides.

"Is that a yes?" he asks.

Before I can answer, Jeremy yells from behind us, "Stop distracting my teammate!"

I startle, realizing where we are. I was so lost in my thoughts of Kiran that I didn't realize I was supposed to be bowling.

I glare back at him in accusation. "You did that on purpose!"

He smirks at me and brings a hand up to his chest. "Who me? Never!"

So I give him a smirk right back. "Tell you what, if I get a strike here, I'll spend the night with you."

He narrows his eyes at me. Now, he probably regrets getting me worked up before I throw.

He steps back, so I line up and throw. It's going a little to the right of the middle and it doesn't appear like it's going to be a strike. Then it curves in, and I swear I see the shadows move as all the pins get knocked down.

I turn and glare at Kiran, and before I can accuse him of anything, he's picking me up and spinning me around. He drops a kiss on my mouth, and I decide to let it go. I'm not even sure I saw anything.

"She's not on our team. Shouldn't you be more upset?" Jay asks, laughing.

"Nah, I definitely won," he says, winking back at me.

I go sit by Jax and Jeremy who are happy we won. Jax takes

my hand when I sit down next to him.

"Another game?" he asks.

I don't want this to end. I'm loving all this time as a group, so I nod yes. Nic goes to set it up, and we play again. This time, Jeremy has gotten better, and we win by a lot. No one complains or gets mad. We just enjoy having fun together, and I love it.

We call it after that game and head back home. As soon as we get in the door, Kiran grabs me and carries me upstairs.

"Goodnight!" I shout over his shoulder to the other guys, who are laughing at Kiran's antics.

Twenty-Seven

Aly

We get up to Kiran's room and he sets me down before making his way over to his bed.

"Come here, baby. I've wanted you all night," Kiran says from his spot on his bed. He's looking at me like I'm a meal he's about to devour.

I take slow steps towards him, drawing out the anticipation. When I'm within reach, he pulls me in, and his lips meet mine immediately. He gives my lips a strong bite as punishment for making him wait but then he's sucking on the spot and soothing the sting away.

I moan into his mouth when his tongue meets mine and we both start attacking each other. Damn, Kiran can kiss. We are completely tangled up together in the bed, limbs everywhere as we try to get as close to each other as possible. He's full of dark chuckles and sexy grins every time he makes me moan louder and louder. The way he's touching my body is pure possessiveness, and I love it. It makes me so hot I can't breathe. I'm pretty sure Kiran owns me right now. He could say jump and I would ask how high to keep getting his drugging kisses.

He could probably convince me to spend the rest of my night here on his bed, making out with him, but he wants more, and so do I. He's on top of me with his hand slowly making its way down my body. He's touching me in sensitive places but pulling away when I react. He finally makes his way to my jeans which he quickly undoes before shoving his hand down my pants. He magically finds my clit right away, and I'm writhing under him as he plays with it.

But I want more, and these damn jeans are in the way. I lift my ass off the bed to shimmy them off and Kiran raises his head to stare me in the eyes. When he realizes what I'm doing, he eases back a little and helps.

Once my jeans are off, he strips his, too, before saying, "Shirt too. I want you naked and under me now, baby."

I comply, stripping everything off until he has full access to my body. He takes advantage right away by plunging two fingers right into me. I scream out and he pumps them a few times before making a come here motion in me that makes me shatter around him. Once I've soaked his fingers, he pulls them out.

I think he's going to replace his fingers with his dick but he surprises me by bringing his fingers back towards my ass and circling. My eyes shoot up to him, and he looks like a king above me.

"What do you think, baby? Want to try? I could get one of the other guys in here to fill your other hole, and we could make you feel so damn good."

It's the idea of having two of them in me that makes me agree.

Aly

I've always been curious, and I've done ass-play in the past. I've used plugs, so I should be nice and ready for him, but I've never let a guy fuck me there. It's only right one of my mates gets the honor of being first.

He slowly pushes a finger, slick with my come, into my ass. I gasp into our kiss, and he chuckles as the gasp turns into a moan. Fuck that feels incredible.

He pushes a second one in and starts scissoring and stretching me out. When he realizes how easy it is, he goes suddenly still and gazes down at me seriously.

"I thought you said you've never been fucked here, baby? Did you lie to me?" he asks and I've never heard Kiran so serious.

"What if I did lie? What if you weren't the first?" I ask, stirring the pot. I can't help myself. I love watching these guys get so damn possessive over me.

He thrusts his fingers back in harder, still stretching and opening me for him, even as he talks.

"Well, I would be pretty mad you didn't save this for me, baby. No other guy gets what belongs to me," he says, almost growling.

"Four other guys in this house get what belongs to you, Kiran. You don't mind that," I point out.

He laughs darkly, and the shadows around us seem to grow bigger and darker as Kiran gets worked up.

"That's different, and you know it. Now tell me who it was so I can go kill them," he grits out through his teeth, pulling his fingers back out of me and lubing up his dick.

I think I've tortured him enough, "No one, Kiran, you'll be my first, I promise. It's only ever been toys, it's all yours for the taking, so take it."

At my challenge, he flips me over, lifts my ass in the air, and plunges into me.

"Fuck!" I scream, and I'm already so damn close.

"That's right, baby, I feel good, don't I?" he taunts, thrusting in and out of me at a measured pace. He's hitting new nerve endings, and it feels incredible. I'm lucky I've used toys before because Kiran is huge.

"So damn good," and because I know it'll make him take me harder, I add, "I'm so glad I waited for you. So you could claim me like this, only you."

And he does. He fucks my ass so hard I'm about to come but my pussy feels so empty.

"You said you were going to share me Kiran, was that a lie so you could have my ass?" I ask.

He doesn't respond, instead fucking me so hard I come and see starts. As I'm coming, he grabs my arm and rolls us so he's under me, and I'm facing up.

When I open my eyes, it's to see Jay gazing down at me with fire in his eyes. He fists my hair and tilts my head to the side so he can devour me with his kisses.

He leans back, taking in my flushed skin and dripping wet pussy.

"Fuck, I'm glad Kiran called me," he says, taking his clothes off until he's naked in front of me.

Kiran leans in to bite my shoulder before saying, "She wanted you, and my baby gets what she wants."

Jay gets on the bed, straddling me from above.

With a nod, he says, "Whatever she wants." Then he slides home. He pushes into me slowly, and I feel so fucking stuffed full, but it's incredible. So many nerves are being stimulated at once and I'm ready to come again already.

He gets going, and Kiran joins him. They alternate their

movements so someone is always inside me. I'm screaming again and I'm sure anyone else who's home knows exactly what we are doing in here.

I come again, and they fuck me right through it. Kiran's hands are a brand on my hips while Jay is still fisting my hair and kissing me like his life depends on it.

"You coming is the hottest damn thing in the world Aly Kat," Jay says.

Kiran pumps into me a few more times before coming with a groan I feel throughout my whole body.

Jay rolls us off Kiran but still manages to be on top as he fucks me savagely into the mattress.

"Say you're mine, Aly Kat," Jay demands.

I comply, "I'm yours, Jay."

He leans towards my neck and gives me a bite, where he sucks a mark into my skin. I'm sure he's leaving teeth marks, but they are not deep enough to break the skin. I trust he won't do that without my permission.

His teeth set me off, and I come around him one final time, setting him off. He growls around my neck in his mouth before collapsing on top of me.

All three of us are breathing heavily. Kiran cleans me up before giving me a soul-deep kiss that I can feel in my toes.

Jay licks the mark on my neck, and I swear he almost purrs.

"How bad is it?" I ask.

Jay gazes up at me, and while he seems mostly pleased with himself, I can tell he's nervous about my reaction.

"It's not so bad," he says, and Kiran scoffs.

"She's going to see it, you idiot, so don't lie."

I look at Jay pointedly, and he fesses up, sounding proud, "Fine, it's huge and dark and so fucking sexy. Everyone will know you're mine now, and I can't feel bad about that. My wolf needed this, Aly Kat. Please don't be mad."

How can I be when he's being so patient about the mate bond? He told me that his wolf has been dying to mark me since we've met. If this makes him feel better and more settled in our relationship, then I'm glad. Plus, it was hot as hell.

I give him a sweet kiss, and he relaxes when he realizes I understand.

They firmly pin me between the two of them, and we settle in to snuggle on the bed, all three of us content.

Twenty-Eight

Aly

Jay and I have been spending a lot of time together making meals. He's been so patient teaching me. I love that we have something just the two of us. He would never let any of the guys into his kitchen, and they know not to try.

We've spent the time together well. We are getting to know each other, asking questions the whole time we cook. I feel close to him and like I'm ready for the next step between us. I'm just not sure when to tell him. I think he has something special planned for tonight so maybe then?

Jay asked me if he could spend time with me tonight, and he seemed extra excited, so I happily agreed. Right now, he is leading me up to his room, almost vibrating with energy.

"Hold on, one minute," he says. He runs into the room ahead of me and shuts the door in my face.

I stand there patiently, wondering why he's being so weird.

Finally, he comes back holding a rose, which he offers to me.

I feel a blush form on my cheeks. Why is he being so romantic?

"What's this for?" I ask.

"I wanted to make you feel special," he responds.

He opens the door, giving me a view of the room. Rose petals are scattered everywhere, including his bed.

I gasp, "Jay, you did all this?"

"Of course, I did it for you, Aly Kat."

I step towards him and stretch up to meet his lips. He lets me control the kiss for a minute before he forces his tongue against mine.

Before the kiss gets too heated, he pulls away. I give him a confused face, but he just grabs my hand and leads me inside. He has two glasses of wine set on his nightstand. He grabs them and offers me one.

"Here's to us, Aly Kat, and our future."

He lifts his glass up to clink it with mine. I can feel myself smiling so hard. I can't believe he did all this for me.

I give him a sultry gaze and lick the rim of my glass. He grabs it from me and sets them both down.

"We can finish these later. Right now I want to taste you."

He picks me up by my thighs and turns to throw me on the bed face down. I bounce a few times before feeling him grab my pants and pull them down.

He takes my panties with them until I'm completely exposed to him. I reach up and remove my shirt and bra, leaving myself completely bare.

I feel his weight settle against me, his front lining up with my back until I can feel his length against me, and his mouth starts kissing my neck. He licks and sucks my neck, I can tell he's leaving marks all along it. I feel dominated by this position, and I love it. He nibbles on my ear lobe, tugging at it.

Aly

He starts slowly moving down my body, kissing, licking, and biting as he goes. I'm sure my spine is going to be covered entirely in teeth marks. I love it, but it's not enough. I want the ultimate mark from him. He has shown me how much I mean to him, and I know how badly he wants to mate me. I want this with Jay like I have with Nic and Kiran.

He gets to the base of my spine before sliding off my body. I miss his weight and heat immediately.

"Jay! Come back," I whimper.

"It's okay, Aly, I'm coming," he responds. I can hear clothes rustling behind me, and suddenly, I feel a very naked body against me.

He must have striped.

"Do you want me, Aly?" he asks in a deep tone.

"Yes, so bad, Jay. I want you so bad," I groan back.

"Are you mine?" He growls, and it sounds like his wolf is coming through.

"Yes, I'm yours!"

He plunges into me hard and fast. His attention to my body making me so wet and ready for him.

He pumps into me a few times before leaning his body over mine and bringing his lips to my ear.

"Yeah, Aly Kat, that's right, you're mine."

He punctuates it with a thrust, and I'm lost for words. All I can do is moan as he hits the best spot in me.

Jay kisses my neck between thrusts, and I have the strongest urge to beg him to bite me right there. I hold off, knowing it'll drive him crazy if I wait to ask him. I'm sure he's wishing for it as he softly bites me there now.

"Damn, every time I think about you, I get hard. Do you know you do that to me?" He groans, pumping into me harder.

"What do you picture doing to me?" I ask.

"Exactly this, but I'm biting and claiming you in my version. I can't control myself around you."

And that's precisely what I want to hear.

"Then do it. Bite me, Jay," I demand.

He growls, and his thrust gets harder, bottoming out in me.

"Don't say that, Aly, or I'll really do it," he warns.

"I know, I want you to, Jay. I want you to bite me, and I want you as my mate," I declare.

"Fuck!"

He pulls my hair, lifting my head and exposing my neck to him. I feel his sharp teeth rake down my throat, and I clench around him.

"You really do want this," he says in wonder.

Before I can respond, sharp teeth break the skin on my neck, and I'm filled with pure ecstasy. Pleasure spreads to every inch of my body from my neck. I shatter around him and feel myself go limp.

"Oh God, Jay!" I shout.

He sucks hard around the spot, leaving a permanent mark on my neck before pulling his teeth loose and finishing in me.

He half collapses on me before leaning back and flipping me over. My body moves, compliant to his demands and completely strung out.

I feel the bond form between us. A connection straight to him from my soul to his. This is the first mate bond I completely understood what was happening as it formed and it feels amazing to enjoy him filling every inch of me.

"That was amazing," I whisper, leaning up to kiss him, even though he's covered in my blood.

"It was, mate," he says.

Aly

A part of me sings at the term. I can feel Jeremy and Nic's shock, happiness, and awe at this bond forming.

I snuggle closer to him, bridging the gap of any space between us.

I want to feel as connected to him as I can right now.

Twenty-Nine

Jeremy

Aly is an incredible fighter and even though we don't know who trained her or why she can't remember it, I'm just glad she can protect herself.

My instincts have calmed down with each bond she's formed and now that she has three of us bonded, I'm feeling more confident in her safety.

She just needs to bond Jax and Kiran and we will all be complete. I have no doubt it's coming soon. I think she'll probably bond with Kiran in the next few days and maybe Jax after they go on a date. They don't need to be intimate to have the bond, so they can continue to wait. I know Aly wants them and Kiran and Jax are probably dying for theirs.

It's training time with Aly, although we should just call it sparring since we aren't training her. If anything, she should be training us, but she can't because of the spell. I'm sure Nic is dying to try to remove any remaining spells but he's being

Jeremy

smart by waiting. We have no idea what will happen and the last time he tried, she almost died. I don't think any of us are looking for a repeat performance.

I have a new idea to try today, to step our sparring up a notch. All the guys have gathered, but I'm going to send them away. This idea only works with me, so they would be a distraction.

"So, I was thinking today we work on weapons and killing blows," I say.

We've used weapons before, and Aly has been a natural at all of them, but we've always been careful not to let anyone get hurt.

"I don't know Jer. Do you think that's a good idea?" Jay asks.

"What are you talking about? I'm not killing anyone!" Aly responds, sounding horrified at the idea.

"Of course not," I say, stepping over and wrapping her up in my arms. "I can't die with these weapons, so you can strike me without worrying."

She's glaring at me like I'm crazy, and I can't hold back my laugh.

"I promise, here," I point to Nic and step away from Aly.

Nic raises his eyebrows, asking if I'm sure, and I nod. This will help make sure Aly is safe, so I'm sure.

He picks up a sword and digs it right into my chest. I barely feel the pain before I fall and black out.

I return to my body in what feels like seconds later, but it was probably a few minutes. Aly is sitting next to me with shock and horror on her face.

"That was terrifying!" she yells before pulling me in for a hug. I can feel the wound healing, and it's like nothing happened.

I glance up to see Nic has a black eye he's healing, clearly Aly didn't take that well.

Bound

"Now you've seen how it works, I can't die like this. It's part of being my kind of demon, let's practice with weapons and you can be less careful. Okay?"

She nods but she looks skeptical. I think it's going to take some pushing but at least she's not outright saying no.

I glance over to the guys. "You should spend this time doing more research on what Aly could be. I can handle training."

Nic nods. "Jax and I will go research. Jay and Kiran will stay and help."

I'm about to complain, we don't need help, but Nic cuts me off with one look. So, instead, I nod.

They head back upstairs, and Kiran and Jay get comfortable in the corner.

I wipe the sword off before handing it to Aly. Then I pick one up myself.

"Let's just start like we normally do, okay?" I ask, and she nods.

We start sparring, our swords clashing, and I know she's holding back. She anticipates my every move, but she doesn't use any of the openings I leave to attack me back.

"Come on, Aly!" Kiran shouts, and Aly pulls a small smile, but her concentration never breaks.

"Yeah, hit him!" Jay adds.

"You're purely on defense right now. Show some offense, I can take it," I demand.

She hesitantly strikes out at me, and I block her easily. The idea that I can protect myself must help because she is starting to attack me.

She gets a few nicks in that bleed but nothing too bad. I don't strike her once, but this is about her getting used to fighting back, not just protecting herself.

Jeremy

We both start to get going, moving around the whole room, and I'm fighting at full strength to protect myself. I leave an easy opening, and she goes for it, slashing my stomach open.

I can feel blood pouring down my stomach, but it's not a killing blow. I can feel my magic starting to heal it already.

She doesn't take her eyes off it until it's healed, and I remind her, "This is good practice for me too. I need to train to protect myself better."

She must agree because she starts up again. This time, when she sees an opening, she plunges the blade through my stomach, and I feel everything start to go dark.

The last thing I hear is Jay and Kiran cheering and maybe someone else saying no? Hopefully, Aly isn't too upset.

Thirty

Ajax

Nic and I head upstairs, back to the pile of books we spend all our free time looking through. I know the mystery is wearing on Aly, and we need to solve it soon. Her powers could emerge at any point, and we need to be prepared. It's probably getting close to the point where we need to ask someone else for help. I know we can trust our parents, but our instincts demand we protect our mate, and telling anyone feels like the wrong move.

Aly is sparring with Jeremy right now. He had a smart idea of practicing harder with weapons. He's the only one of us who can be 'killed,' and then come back. He only dies when a particular metal is used, which, luckily, we don't keep around.

It's important for Aly to practice actual killing moves. We don't know what's coming after her and she might have to take that step for her survival one day. It's most important to me that she stays safe. Kiran and Jay are keeping an eye on them and making sure everything goes okay. It was hard to

Ajax

walk away but it's more important we find something than just watch them spar.

Nic and I are combing through more books, looking for the answer to Aly's mating mark. That's the easiest clue to go by, but we might have to try something else soon. We still haven't figured out what she could be, but it's clear she's something supernatural to have her own mating mark.

I'm on what feels like my hundredth book. This one is ancient and was hard to get my hands on, almost impossible. I start looking through it when surprising even myself, I see the mark. Right there in the book are the arrows crossing each other in red on someone's chest.

"Nic, here it is!" I shout, getting his attention. This is huge! Hopefully, there's more here to help us.

Nic shoots out of his seat and comes to peer over my shoulder.

The book reads *This ancient mating mark has not been seen in hundreds of years as mating with hunters has become nonexistent.*

I am shocked down to my core, and based on his silence, I'm sure Nic is, too.

"A... a hunter? She can't be a hunter. She would have never gotten this close to us or mated with us! How could a hunter be our fated mate?" I'm scrambling with all these questions but it just doesn't make any sense.

"Well, it looks like hundreds of years ago, supernaturals did mate with hunters. Otherwise, there would be no record of the mark," Nic adds slowly like he's trying to catch up to his thinking.

"So, if hunters mated with other supernaturals, they may not automatically hate us. It could be something else that drives them to hunt our kind," I say.

Bound

"Aly has never shown even a hint of hating us or what we are. If anything, she's been incredibly positive," Nic adds.

He's right. "Hunter or not, she's still our Aly and our mate. We will just have to figure out what this means for us."

"You're right, it's going to be hard to tell her," Nic adds. And he's right. All we've been doing is talking badly about hunters and encouraging her to learn how to protect herself from them. She's going to think we hate her, but we could *never* hate her.

I try to think of everything I know about hunters. It's not much, they're incredibly secretive. We will have to find any books we can to help Aly, but I don't even know where to start. I wonder if some of the guys know more than I do.

All I know is…

"Wait! I know hunter culture isn't shared outside hunter families, but don't you have to trigger your hunter gene?" I don't like where my thought process is going.

"Oh, shit. Killing a supernatural triggers the gene!" Nic looks downstairs, worried, before taking off in a sprint.

I follow closely behind. We have to stop Aly and Jeremy before she makes the kill. This could trigger her to change into a full hunter and make everything harder. She should at least have the choice!

Ahead of me, Nic shouts, "No!" Trying to stop anything from happening.

Before we make it, a loud pop echoes through the house.

Sliding to a stop inside the training room, I bump into Nic.

Aly is standing there in complete shock as another mark makes its way around her neck. It's a blood-red choker with two crossed arrows in the center. It's all sharp edges and bold lines, the mark of a hunter. I can't believe I never connected the dots, no wonder the mark was so familiar. But without the context, none of us realized.

Next to Aly is the source of the pop. An older version of Aly is standing there staring with a disapproving glare. She has Aly's same brown hair but is slightly taller and much more built. Lines around her eyes and mouth betray her age.

Staring up at the woman, Aly whispers, confirming my suspicions, "Mom?"

Her eyes sweep the room, taking all of us in. She knows what we are. She peers down at Jeremy's body on the ground before bringing her attention back to Aly.

I'm terrified. We have a real-life hunter in our house—a hunter who is standing dangerously close to my mate, even if it is her mom. Nic takes a step closer, clearly worried about Aly, too.

"Oh, Aly dear, what have you done?" The mom shakes her head, furious.

Then, she grabs my mate's arm and they both disappear with a pop. We all lunge forward, but there's nothing we can do.

One second, she's right here with us, and the next, she's gone.

* * *

Want to know what happens next? Check out book three in the series, Break, on Amazon!

About the Author

Thank you for reading! The fact that you have read my book makes my day. I'm a newer author and I hope you really enjoyed the book. If you enjoyed the story and want to hear more, consider writing a review! Reviews are essential to helping more people find books they will love and are the best encouragement for me to keep writing! I look forward to hearing what you think!

Keep up to date with me by subscribing to my mailing list, joining my Facebook reader group, or following me on social media.
I am an indie author living in Colorado with my dog Bentley. She is my favorite writing companion but she loves to distract me when I'm in a groove! I have always loved to write and had stories rolling around in my head, so I recently decided to write some books and see where it takes me. Thanks for joining me on this adventure!

You can connect with me on:
🌐 https://linktr.ee/D.M.Page

Subscribe to my newsletter:
✉ https://mailchi.mp/5ac6d54c287f/welcome

Also by D.M. Page

Break (Brickstone University Reverse Harem Book 3)
On Amazon

Aly has been taken and the guys need to get her back before they lose it completely. Nicoli, Jeremy, Jay, Kiran and Ajax are lost without their mate and will do anything to get her back. Once they do, they'll do anything to keep her safe from those who took her.

This is a medium burn, paranormal, reverse harem, meaning she doesn't have to choose and book three of four in the series. The story changes POVs between the main character and her men. The steaminess factor will go up as the series goes on and is intended for 17+. This is 45,000 words and ends on a cliff hanger

Off The Rush
Find it on Amazon

A standalone!

When the biggest audition of Emma's college career is rudely interrupted by a hockey player, she'll do anything to fix it. Including, fake dating that hockey player.

She never expects it will mean spending so much time with him and his sexy roommates. They're always there flirting, teasing, and bringing her into their tight-knit fold. It's dangerous when her feelings keep growing for all of them.

Alec is on thin ice with his coach and needs to convince him he's settling down or risk losing his spot on the team. The solution comes to him in the form of a music major asking for something crazy.
When Alec's roommates and fellow hockey players, JD and Luka meet Emma, sparks fly quickly leading to jealousy.

The boys can't agree on what to do. It's not the first time, but this decision is make or break. Every single one of them is obsessed with Emma and every second together makes their feelings grow stronger.

*This is a full-length 100,000 word contemporary standalone why choose hockey romance with lots of spice and a guaranteed

happily ever after*

Captive (Forgotten Gods Reverse Harem Romance)
On Amazon

Complete series!

I was a normal girl, until one day I wasn't. The very same day, men stole me away and held me captive. They imprisoned me with four guys, all with powers of their own: Apollo, Ares, Hephaestus and Hermes. They keep me sane while we plot our escape. But will we make it out alive?

This is a medium burn, paranormal prison fantasy, reverse harem. The story changes POVs between the main character and her men. The steaminess factor will go up as the series goes on and is intended for 17+. This is a short novella for the first book, 30,000 words and ends on a cliffhanger

For One Night
Available on Amazon

Halloween is the night ghosts get to roam the streets and live like a human. Micaela is planning to enjoy her night to the fullest when she meets three paranormals: a vampire, a werewolf and a warlock.

What happens when your fated mate is a ghost who only gets to be corporal for one night? You find a way to keep her.

Will they be able to or will they lose their fated mate after only one night?

This is a fast burn, paranormal, why choose romance, meaning she doesn't have to choose between the love interests. This is a standalone novella. The story changes POVs between the main character and her men. This is a steamy story and is intended for 18+. This is 30,000 words.

Changed
Anna's story starts in book one of the Alpha Team Series- Changed. I recommend finishing the Brickstone Series before looking at Anna's as it will contain spoilers!

On Amazon

Excerpt from Captive

"Can I have this loaf of bread?" I ask, holding up a bag of sourdough. The vendor locks eyes with me immediately. Usually, this man would ogle my body before answering my question but today his gaze doesn't leave my eyes.

"Yes of course," he responds, sounding almost robotic. Maybe he's distracted by something else.

I reach into my purse and hand him a ten-dollar bill. He doesn't even glance down at the money or reach out for it. He doesn't even acknowledge that I'm trying to pay him.

"Here yeah go," I try again, practically waving the money in front of his face. He doesn't break eye contact, just continues staring at me.

I give him a minute to get out of his head and realize he's too distracted to accept payment. The sweet scent of food drifts up from all around me covering the smell of fish off the ocean.

"You have the loaf of bread," he answers my attempt to give him money.

Is he really giving this bread to me? I shop at this farmers market every Saturday and this vendor has never once given me something for free. Usually, he's an absolute crab who can't be bothered to have a conversation.

"You don't want money?" I ask, once again trying to pay him. He doesn't respond just staring at me, "Okay, thank you!" I watch him as I walk away, making sure he's really giving me this bread.

It's not like I'm rolling in money so I can't afford to turn down a gift. Maybe the universe is trying to wish me a happy birthday.

Shouts break out all around me but I can't see what the

commotion is. I ignore everything, making my way through the market. The further I walk the louder the scene gets, demanding my attention.

Turning around, I see people jumping out of the way in all directions. Whatever the problem is, it's coming towards me.

Three men in black are pushing everyone out of the way, heading in my direction. I move to the left, trying to hide behind a booth. I don't want anything to do with this, I don't need more trouble in my life.

The men shift directions, following my movement. Are they following me? They can't be but just to be sure, I take off in a new direction, turning and running. They start running too.

My feet smack the pavement as I push with all my might to get around the next corner. I've gained some ground on these guys and now I need to lose them. Why the hell someone is chasing me in the first place, I have no idea.

One minute I'm charming the guy selling bread at the farmers market, the next, three guys in all black are charging at me. I was just trying to make myself a decent meal for my birthday but I guess fate has other plans.

Today, according to my license, is my twenty-first birthday. Considering I can't remember anything before I was sixteen and out on my own, I can't be sure. I treat it like my birthday, that's all that matters.

Considering they're still chasing me, I guess I can be sure they're after me.

I have always been fast but right now, with adrenaline running through my system, it feels like I'm running at an unbelievable speed. I guess when fight or flight kicks in you really start to feel like you could fly.

As I round another corner arms wrap around me, jolting

my progress to an immediate stop. I fight to get away from another man dressed in all black.

"You're a pretty one, aren't you? I almost don't want to bring you in, almost," Then he shouts, "Got her!" I guess my looks aren't getting me out of this one.

I fight against this guy and I feel a million times stronger than I ever have. I've been in dangerous situations before but never has my adrenaline worked this well. I elbow him right in the gut and he gives a satisfying grunt. With satisfaction, I bring my fist back into his nose, feeling blood spatter everywhere.

"You bitch!" He muffles through his broken nose. It sounds broken.

I don't care if this asshole thinks I'm a bitch, I'm getting the fuck out of here. I turn to run again when a jolt of electricity shocks through my body. It's never-ending, making me feel like I'm going to burn to a crisp from the inside. My knees smack the cold cement hard as I fall forward into a twitching mess. One of the men above leans forward leering at me as he shacks gold cuffs around my wrists.

At the never-ending pain, my vision starts to dim until there is only blackness.

I wake up to the thrum of a car. Assessing my surroundings I feel the velvet of the trunk floor under my cheek. My whole body groans with any movement, it feels like I was hit by a bus. Everything starts coming back in waves, the farmers market, the men in black chasing me, the taser.

What the hell have I gotten myself into? Why have these guys kidnapped me? I start to feel panic creeping up my chest and my breathing quickens. I have no idea what they are planning to do to me but it can't be anything good.

The trunk feels smaller, I'm not getting enough oxygen with

each breath. I'm panicking but I need to get it together. I can't survive this if I'm a shriveling mess, a damsel in distress.

I am stronger than this, I have been through worse than this and survived. That might be a lie but it's a lie I'm sticking with. I take a deep, centering breath, trying to remember what I've read about escaping a moving car. There should be a release somewhere inside the trunk.

Feeling all around me, I find the cord but it's cut. Smart kidnappers, they took that option away from me. I don't know how long I've been passed out or in the car, how far from downtown we've gone.

The car comes to a sudden stop ramming me against the back of the trunk. My body screams at me from another injury. Pain is radiating through my whole body. If we've stopped, I need to prepare for a fight. But I'm in no condition, I can barely lift my arms let alone throw a punch.

My eyes burn from the sun shining in as the trunk opens revealing my captors. It's two men staring down at me. One is burly, the other lanky. They're two sides of a coin, I guess that's why they're partners.

"Oh look, the bitch is up," the man above me caresses my cheek as he ogles my chest. Burly. Clearly, he is a disgusting pig, I've been stared at my entire life and nothing has felt as creepy as this man.

He lifts me over his shoulder, into a fireman's carry. I try to look around from my upside-down position. Dizziness rushes over me, turning my vision dark. I feel nauseous, my stomach revolting from being thrown around. There is no stopping my stomach from emptying itself on the back of the man holding me.

"Fucking bitch!"

Does this guy really not have any other insults in his vocabulary than bitch?

Surprisingly, after emptying my stomach my vision starts to clear and I can finally take in my surroundings.

We are outside what looks like a compound. Tall cement walls with no windows. The place looks abandoned from the outside. I can't smell the ocean anymore so we must be far from the coast.

I know with certainty that if they get me inside there, I'm not getting out. It's a feeling deep in my soul. This isn't a question the captive then let her go kind of situation. There isn't a happy ending to this place.

I need to fight. I go to strike out against my captor but it feels like my arms are made of jello. Every movement makes my injuries worse. Clearly, when they caught me they made sure I was going to stay down. These injuries can't all be from the taser they hit me with.

My arms have no strength, my right arm feels like it might be broken. I can barely get air into my lungs, each breath causing a sharp pain deep in my chest. My leg feels broken, every step this man takes jostles my injuries, making them worse.

"Don't even try Doll Face, those cuffs drain you of all your strength and powers."

That explains why my body feels like jello but what does he mean by powers? This guy is mental if he thinks I have any type of power.

"Is that why you took me? Do you think I have powers? I swear I don't, you can let me go. I won't tell anyone about this." My raspy voice sounds pathetic even to me but I have to try.

"Good try, but we saw you at the market and we've been tracking you since this morning." The lanky one responds before putting duct tape over my mouth, silencing any further protests.

As he carries me in I'm still mumbling through my duct tape. There's no one around for miles but I can't just give up.

We get to the door, lanky scanning his key card before opening it. Burly carries me inside.

The inside of the building looks like a laboratory. It's cleaner and more well-kept than I would have expected from the outside. The whole place reeks of bleach and there are guards everywhere. I'm trying to take in every detail I can, already planning my escape.

Lanky takes a step behind us and before I can hide my interest he realizes what I'm doing. A second later there's a hard hit to my head and everything goes black.

Want to know what happens next?

Find it on Amazon